# STRIPPER

# STRIPPER

A Romance Novel

*Dawn Splendour*

iUniverse, Inc.
New York Lincoln Shanghai

# Stripper
## A Romance Novel

All Rights Reserved © 2003 by Dawn Splendour

iUniverse, Inc.

For information address:
iUniverse, Inc.
2021 Pine Lake Road, Suite 100
Lincoln, NE 68512
www.iuniverse.com

ISBN: 0-595-29026-4

Printed in the United States of America

# Contents

# CHAPTER 1

# *Graduation Day*

As Michelle toweled herself off after her shower, the bathroom mirror reflected the image of a beautiful eighteen-year old girl: she was somewhat above average height, with a cascade of golden hair, a happy face, full breasts, strong arms and shoulders, a firm tummy, a tight little fanny, and long, slim legs, all enclosed in a creamy skin. A perky brush of reddish-gold hair asserted itself at the junction.

Michelle thought nothing of it. This was the body given her at birth, and while growing up she had paid little attention to it. She had always been healthy and happy. She knew that she looked good in school clothes, work clothes, and party clothes, and that gave her the confidence to be herself. That was all.

Michelle was a winsome teenager, who enjoyed each day to the fullest. June 5, 1999, was an especially happy day, because she would graduate from Clarksville High School. The ceremony would take place at 10:00 a.m. in the outdoor arena by the football field. The weather was perfect for commencement and promised a warm, pleasant evening for the party at the lake, where the graduates could enjoy their newfound freedom and blow off a little steam.

As a graduation present, Dad had given Michelle the diamond necklace and ear-rings that her mother had worn for special occasions. Michelle put on her bathrobe, wrapped her head in a towel, and stepped into her bath slippers. She returned to her bedroom and walked to the dressing table where the necklace and ear-rings sparkled in the early morning light. The jewelry brought back memories of her mother, who had been a Philadelphia socialite from a prominent Main Line family.

Mom was tall, blonde, and slim, and an avid horsewoman. She had met Dad through their mutual interest in Arabian horses. Despite her eastern upbringing and Bryn Mawr education, Mom was a homebody, who had immediately accepted the prairies of Illinois. She taught Michelle the art of horsemanship, and by the time she was ten Michelle was winning prizes in competitions throughout northern and central Illinois, including the Illinois State Fair in Springfield.

Together, Dad and Mom had made Plainfield Arabians famous throughout America, Europe, and the Middle East. Dad traveled the world, meeting and dealing with horse people. Mom entertained beautifully the buyers who came from far and wide to buy horses.

Mom had been a working horsewoman, who did not disdain the hard physical labor that came with horses: feeding, grooming, and cleaning up after them. More than once she had thrust her arm into a mare's birth canal and helped the foal into the light of day. One time her arm was broken by the contractions of the mare. When Michelle was twelve, Mom died from complications arising from a fall from a horse.

As Michelle dawdled, lost in her memories, Thelma came bustling into the bedroom. She was a lean, wiry, blunt-spoken, down-to-earth Irish woman from the south side of Chicago, who had come to look after Michelle and the house after Mom died. She always referred to Michelle as "Mickey," the family nickname, and perhaps Michelle served as a substitute for the children that Thelma never had.

She helped Michelle slip into a light, flowered summer dress to wear under her graduation gown. Michelle gathered her long golden hair into a fetching ponytail. Thelma was well aware of Michelle's blossoming beauty, and insisted on making the most of it by helping Michelle dress for special occasions.

"I wasn't much of a looker meself," she would mutter, "but I like to see good looks made the most of."

Dad knocked his special little knock and stepped into the room.

"C'm here, baby," he said, giving Michelle a hug. "Let me put on your mother's jewelry. She was beautiful, you know. She made the jewels look good—not the other way around."

"You make them look beautiful too," he whispered, as he fastened the necklace.

"When the time comes," he added, "you can wear these. But not yet."

Michelle turned and gave her father a squeeze.

"You're a wonderful Daddy," she said.

Dad was of average height, slim and dapper, with a pencil mustache. He looked every bit the polished gentleman and sportsman. His cosmopolitan charm made him welcome in the highest social circles. One of his proudest achievements was to sell a colt to a member of the British royal family, Princess Anne, a superb equestrienne who had competed in the Olympic Games. After her mother's death, Michelle's love was focused on Dad. In her youthful dreams of love and happiness, Dad provided the masculine ideal.

They heard a honk outside the open window. Uncle Jim and Aunt Chloe were driving them to the graduation in their new SUV. Thelma refused to go. She said landmark events, like graduations, weddings, and funerals, always made her cry.

"Have a good time," she said, tears welling up in her eyes. "My little girl is growing up, and soon she will leave me for some man."

She pronounced the word "man" with a combination of exasperation and contempt.

As they approached the outdoor arena, it was apparent that all of Clarksville was turning out. People were streaming in from every direction. When Uncle Jim had parked the car, Michelle took her cap and gown and headed for the robing area where the graduates were preparing for the processional. Dad went with Uncle Jim and Aunt Chloe to the rows of folding chairs reserved for parents and friends. Luke, Lena, and Ben, employees at Plainfield, sat farther back.

Michelle was popular among her classmates, and had been chosen Homecoming Queen the previous October. Her good looks did not inspire envy, because she was pleasant and cheerful to everyone. Her closest friend, Clara, and Clara's boyfriend, Rusty, were also graduating. Since she did not have playmates living nearby, from childhood Michelle had spent Saturdays in town with Clara. She was thrilled that Clara and Rusty were getting married the next weekend, and she would be the bridesmaid.

The girls were shoved aside by Sonny Grubbs, captain of the football and basketball teams and Big Man on Campus—in his own estimation, anyway. Since he was Number One guy, and everyone recognized Michelle as Number One girl, the high school pecking order dictated that he lay claim to her. Michelle was not interested in dating, and she felt no need for a boyfriend. She was satisfied to pal around with her classmates, but at school activities Sonny simply stepped up and took over. Michelle did not like Sonny's crude and domineering ways, but he let the other guys know that Michelle was his, and no one dared challenge him.

There was one classmate who tried—Waldo Smart, the class nerd. As Michelle marched with her classmates into the arena, the school band playing "Pomp and Circumstance," she saw that Waldo was on the dais with the dignitaries. Waldo was valedictorian and would present the class farewell. The local paper had announced that he had a scholarship to Cal Tech, and would be leaving shortly after graduation to take up residence.

Waldo was tall and lanky, with a head too big for his yet undeveloped body, and hands too big for his skinny arms. Despite being poorly coordinated and unathletic, Waldo played center on the basketball team, where his height enabled him to make dunks, get rebounds, and block shots. Sonny Grubbs, of course, was the star and main scorer, although he often fouled out in the last quarter, when he was most needed.

Waldo was shy and uncomfortable with most of his classmates, especially the girls. He was said to be a whiz with computers. Michelle liked and respected Waldo's brains and industriousness. When Waldo had awkwardly asked her to go with him to the party at the lake, she turned him down as politely as she could. Sonny expected her to go with him, and she didn't want trouble with Sonny at this point.

"Some other time," she said to Waldo, trying to sound encouraging. Sadly she realized that he was leaving soon, and some other time would probably never come.

After the graduation, the family returned to Plainfield Farm for lunch, and then Uncle Jim and Aunt Chloe returned home. Michelle took off her graduation dress, and got into the blue denim shirt and jeans that she wore while working with the horses. At the moment, the farm had two brood mares, two colts, two fillies, three geldings, and Akbar, a young and sometimes obstreperous stallion. Sales were pending for three of the geldings and one filly. The horses were in the paddock, or turnout lot, where they crowded to the gate as Michelle approached.

Arabians need love and attention from their masters, and give the same abundantly in return. Fatima, the eldest mare, led the way. She was near the end of her fertility. At her side was Sibyl, her filly, now of the proper age to be bred and bear young. Akbar, the young stallion, whose sense of male dignity required that he not look too eager, took his time in joining his harem in crowding around Michelle.

Akbar and Sybil were the future of Plainfield. Akbar was a descendant of the great "Godolphin" stallion, brought to England in the eighteenth century, and progenitor of many great Arabians. Sybil exhibited to perfection the characteristics of the Arabian horse: small ears, a delicate nose with a slight dip in it, wide nostrils, large jawbone, long neck, a shorter back than other breeds, and a sociable nature. She would not be sold, but would be kept as a brood mare, replacing her mother, who would live out the rest of her life grazing the green pastures of Plainfield.

Living in the country, with her mother dead, her father often absent, and no brothers or sisters, Michelle's best friends, apart from Clara, were the horses. She was with them every day, morning and evening, and sometimes in between. As she passed among the small, sensitive Arabians, Michelle greeted each by name. She stroked them lovingly along their slim necks, backs, and flanks. They understood, by her touch, that this was a special day for her, and shared her joy.

Akbar lacked the female sensitivity of the mares. He knew only three roles: protector of his harem against strangers, warrior against enemies and predators, and detached observer of his inferiors. He made no effort to lead the other horses, a task beneath his dignity: that was the responsibility of Fatima, the senior mare. Additionally, Akbar still retained vestiges of what Michelle called his "big baby mood." He was reluctant to recognize any female as his master, but he accepted Michelle as a surrogate mother. This time Akbar was in his "big baby mood" and cuddled close, welcoming her caresses.

The June evening was warm and the air was heavy with humidity. The setting sun was bright orange, but dark streaks on the horizon carried the threat of a thunderstorm. The party at the lake was to begin at sundown. It was intended to proclaim the independence of the graduates from the structured, adult-controlled world of school to the imagined freedom of grown-ups. There was no planning or organization, and, of course, there were no chaperones. Although under age, Sonny had contrived to obtain a keg of beer, and someone brought pretzels and paper cups. Others brought boom boxes, all of which were tuned to rock radio WLS-Chicago. Everyone brought blankets, because there seemed to be general agreement that this was to be "make-out night."

Michelle was not interested in making out. She had nothing to prove to anyone, and she had firmly resisted Sonny's insistence on physical intimacies. When Sonny arrived at Plainfield to take her to the party, Michelle saw that he was in an ugly mood. His hanger-on, Squirt Peterson, who did not have a girl with him, accompanied him. Like many of the second-rank guys, Squirt was waiting to see who was left over after the first-rank guys had taken their pick.

Sonny's bad temper had been aggravated by the prominence of Waldo at commencement. Sonny was accustomed to being the center of attention. During Waldo's valedictory address he had directed a series of disparaging comments to any of the graduates who would listen.

Sonny was especially irritated with Michelle, who had yet to allow him to prove his masculinity. Sonny had already written "I fucked Michelle" in several johns, but a sense of inadequacy lingered until he had actually performed the deed. He had already announced his intention to Squirt and several of their buddies, and he had decided that he would not take "No" for an answer.

When they arrived at the party, Sonny and Squirt triumphantly set the beer on a stump, to the cheers of their classmates. Officiously Sonny took responsibility for tapping the keg, where he proved to be less experienced than he claimed. As the beer flowed, Michelle noticed nervously that Sonny was downing one cup of beer after another. He pulled her through the gathering with him, talking loudly as he toasted the football team and sang the fight song. He laughed as he shouted the old grade school chant: "No more teachers, No more books, No more teacher's cross eyed looks," naming the teachers and replacing "cross eyed" with more pungent terms. Michelle did not like beer, or the dizzy feeling it gave her, so she stuck to 7-Up and pretzels.

Suddenly Sonny jerked her arm and shoved her along a dim path that led into the trees. "O.K, you little bitch," he muttered, "you've been stringing me along long enough. Now you're going to put out." With that he gave a nod to Squirt, who was trailing a few paces behind. He seized Michelle, pulled her face to his, and began kissing her violently.

Startled by this sudden onset, Michelle resisted as best she could, but Sonny was strong and wrestled her to the ground. He thrust his powerful body between her legs and put one hand over her mouth. With the other hand he pulled down her slacks and underwear. She felt his finger probing her crotch. Squirt seized her flailing arms and pinned them to the ground. As Sonny struggled to open his trousers and lower his shorts, Michelle bit his hand. He reacted with a slap and a curse, which gave Michelle the opportunity to let out a scream. Shouts came from the assembled group, and footsteps were heard approaching them.

The first to appear was Waldo, who pulled Sonny off Michelle's body. Squirt hastily disappeared into the trees, freeing her arms. Clara and Rusty, who had been looking for Michelle, arrived on the scene. Rusty helped Waldo subdue the enraged Sonny, while Clara dropped to the ground and held Michelle in her arms.

Michelle was choking and gasping for air. She remained on her back as Clara put her underwear and slacks back in place. Sonny shook off his tormentors, pulled up his pants, and stalked back to his car. In his view, he had done what a man needed to do, and he was proud of it. Squirt joined him at the car and they drove off.

No one called the police or an ambulance; they represented the adult world of structure, procedures, and punishments. Disheveled guys and girls stumbled out of the woods, talked quietly among themselves, and went home. They passed off Sonny's attack as a lovers' scuffle, not an attempted rape.

Waldo and Rusty helped Michelle into Rusty's pickup, while Clara squeezed in beside her, talking softly to the sobbing girl. "He was like an animal", Michelle moaned. "He hates me. I could see it in his eyes. He hates me. What did I do to bring this on?"

"You didn't do anything," Clara said. "You didn't do anything. Sonny did it, all by himself."

When they arrived at Plainfield the lights were on in the house, and Uncle Jim and Aunt Cloe were waiting for them on the veranda. They were surprised to see Michelle looking badly shaken, walking slowly and supported by Clara and Rusty.

Tenderly Aunt Chloe took Michelle's hands and looked into her eyes.

"Mickey," she said, "I have terrible news. Your father has just had a bad heart attack. There is nothing that we or anyone else can do for him. The county ambulance took him to the hospital emergency room. They called back a few minutes ago and said that he was dead."

At that point Michelle collapsed. Uncle Jim and Rusty carried her to her bedroom, where Clara began undoing Michelle's clothes. Michelle regained consciousness and shakily put on her nightdress. She stumbled into her bathroom and drank a glass of water. Then she returned and collapsed into her bed, shivering violently although it was a warm night.

"Don't go away, Clara," she said. "Please stay with me. Please."

Clara took off her shoes and lay down on the bed in her clothes. They cuddled, as they had done at sleepovers when they were children. Michelle immediately dropped off into a deep, dreamless sleep, while Clara lay awake, wondering what to do next. Eventually she drifted into sleep too, her thin, wiry little body providing warmth and comfort to her orphaned and violated friend.

In the barn, the Arabians were restless, as thunder crashed and lightning flashed across the sky. Then the rain came in sheets. Akbar sensed something else: danger to his mistress. He held his head and ears alert, seeking signs of an enemy. Frustrated, he stamped his feet and rattled his stall. Little Sybil clung closely to her mother, while Fatima uttered comforting sounds to the other horses.

# CHAPTER 2

# *Dad*

In the excitement caused by her father's sudden death, Sonny's brutal assault on Michelle was overlooked. Thelma, who had not seen Michelle arrive home, thought that the girl's obvious distress was solely a reaction to her the death of her father. Michelle was so ashamed that she refused to talk about the party. The next morning Thelma noticed her bruised face and an ugly purple swelling at the edge of one eye. Michelle would not respond to her questions, insisting that nothing had happened except some roughness playing touch football. She felt unworthy to enter a holy place, and used her grief as a reason not to go to church.

When Waldo stopped by later that day to inquire about Michelle, Thelma's suspicions were further aroused. Michelle asked Thelma to thank Waldo, but she refused to come to the door. Michelle felt so degraded that she could not face Waldo, who had seen with his own eyes her humiliation and nakedness. Waldo left for California later that day.

Clara attended church with her parents. Rusty usually went with them, but that morning he had to work at the gas station. After the service Rev. Orval Wiseman, the genial pastor, asked Clara about Michelle. He intended to visit Michelle that evening to express his regrets at her father's death. Clara hesitated for a moment, and then told him that something terrible had happened at the party. The look on Clara's face convinced the clergyman that he should look into the matter further.

"Please wait a few minutes," he said to Clara, "until I am finished here. I want to know more about this."

In the pastor's study Clara gave him a full account of Sonny's attack on Michelle.

"Michelle is really shook up by this," Clara said. "I stayed with her all night, and when I left this morning she didn't want to get out of bed. She just lies there like a lump."

"Clara," Rev. Wiseman replied, "your love and encouragement are much needed. Please stay close to Michelle. You should expect that this experience will continue to haunt her for some time. Furthermore, it appears to me that a serious crime may have been committed. It may be necessary to bring the law into this matter."

"Oh, I know Michelle wouldn't want to be involved in any trial or anything like that," Clara said. "She doesn't want to talk about it at all."

"We won't worry about that now," Rev. Wiseman replied. "All I want to do is find out what happened. At present Michelle probably needs spiritual counsel more than anything. Let me handle it."

That evening Rev. Wiseman stopped at Plainfield, unannounced. He told Thelma that he felt that he should speak to Michelle concerning the death of her father. Thelma welcomed his arrival, but expressed doubt that Michelle would see him. The only person that Michelle would see, Thelma said, was Clara, who had spent all afternoon in Michelle's room. She informed the pastor of the bruises incurred during the party, and expressed her concern at Michelle's emotional state.

Rev. Wiseman knew the house well. Without waiting for an invitation, he stepped in the door and began walking briskly down the hallway. Thelma hurried along behind him. When they reached Michelle's room, Thelma knocked at the door, opened it, and looked in. Michelle was lying on her bed, staring at the ceiling.

Rev. Wiseman stepped into the room and announced his presence. Thelma followed. Rev. Wiseman had married Dad and Mom, and had baptized and confirmed Michelle. He knew his duty as a pastor, and he was determined to do it. Michelle, feeling herself unfit to face a man of God, turned toward the wall.

"Michelle," the pastor said, softly, "I have come to talk to you about your father."

Michelle did not reply.

"Michelle," he continued, "I know how much you loved and admired your father. I also know how much he loved and admired you. As his pastor, I discussed many things with your father that you do not know about. Whatever mistakes he may have made, I know that he was a child of God and will receive the blessings of God's promises."

At that point Michelle burst into tears, and sobs racked her body. Wisely, the good pastor allowed her to vent her sense of hurt and loss. When the tears were exhausted and the sobbing had ceased, he brought up a delicate topic.

"Michelle," he said, "I want to talk to you about the party last night. I have reason to think that you have been the victim of sexual assault, a crime formerly called rape. If true, this crime must be investigated and punished."

"You are not at fault," he added. "You are still the same wonderful girl that you have always been. You are as pure in the eyes of God—and, I will add, my own eyes—as you always were. Please believe me."

"You will have lots of bad feelings about yourself; that is one of the evil consequences of sexual assault. Please let me help you work your way through them."

Rev. Wiseman rose to leave.

"Dear young woman," he said, "you need help that I cannot provide. I will call Dr. Carey in the morning, and ask him to stop by and give you a physical examination. I will also call Lawyer Smart and tell him about my suspicion of sexual assault. Doubtless he will get back to you. And you will have to get ready for your father's funeral, which is set for Tuesday afternoon. Your Uncle Jim has agreed to make arrangements."

"I won't see you until the funeral," the pastor concluded. "Put your faith in God, yourself, and your many friends. G'bye."

The next morning Dr. Carey drove up to the house in his worn little Escort. Dr. Aloyisius Carey was English by birth and training, and he maintained the English tradition of house calls. He was a round, cheery little man, who had practiced medicine in Clarksville for thirty years. He had delivered Michelle and had attempted, unsuccessfully, to save her mother. He was known throughout the area for his willingness to come, day or night.

Although Michelle was rarely ill, she knew and liked Dr. Carey, who came to the school to perform mandatory physical examinations and immunizations. He noted carefully Michelle's cuts and bruises, and prescribed an antibiotic to ward off infections. His examination of the vaginal area was especially careful. He explained that a serious crime had possibly been committed, and that he might be called upon to give evidence.

"As a doctor," he explained, "I am required by law to report any signs of a crime. However," he added, "the physical indicators are not sufficient by themselves to suggest that a charge of sexual assault is in order. I will save the results of my examination until the proper time."

Coaxed by the doctor, Michelle was finally able to tell her story to someone other than Clara. Painfully, she struggled to recall details that her mind had attempted to suppress.

"You must recognize and admit the violence that has been inflicted upon you," Dr. Carey said.

"That is the first step toward recovery."

That afternoon, Michelle had surprise visitors. A Cadillac rental car pulled up in front of the house, and a well-dressed couple in their mid-sixties stepped out. The man was tall and distinguished, with a confident bearing, silvery hair, and a well-tailored summer suit. His wife wore a broad hat, a flowing summer dress, and white shoes. When she answered the door, Thelma did not recognize them, although they acted as if they belonged there.

"We are Michelle's grandparents, from Philadelphia," the lady said. "We have been informed that Michelle's father is dead, and she is now an orphan. We came right away to see her. Will you please inform her that we are here?"

Mom's parents had been deeply disappointed when their daughter married Dad, and came to northern Illinois to raise Arabian horses. With her tall good looks, Bryn Mawr education, and warm personality, they had expected that their daughter would marry into the East Coast elite and continue to be part of their social circle. They disliked Dad, whom they regarded as an opportunist and a social climber. They had come to Plainfield only twice: for Michelle's baptism and Mom's funeral. They had decided that they would not be welcome at the graduation.

Mom had remained close to her parents. Every December, when the horse business was slow, she took Michelle to Philadelphia for a visit, which also included a trip to New York City to visit other relatives and see the Christmas decorations. Michelle had enjoyed those visits enormously. They stopped when Mom died.

Michelle's spirits rose when Thelma announced that her grandparents had come to see her. She quickly put on a dressing gown and hurried to meet them.

"Grandma, Grandpa," she cried, "I'm so glad you came! Oh, I've had such a terrible time! Please stay a while. Dad's dead; I've got to look after Plainfield and the horses; there is so much to do."

She did not tell them about the party and Sonny.

"Michelle, dear," Grandma said, "we can't stay long. And I'm afraid we can't help you much with Plainfield. As to the horses, your mother loved them, but I don't know where she got that. We certainly aren't horsy people."

Grandpa stepped into the conversation.

"Michelle," he said, "we are here to show our love for you at this difficult time. We loved your mother dearly, and we love you too. Every year we looked forward to your visits. Unfortunately, they stopped when your mother died."

He took her hand, and turned her around in a complete circle.

"Let us get a good look at you," he said. "You have grown into a lovely young woman. We have missed you so."

"Please sit down, dear," Grandma said. "We need to talk. We will go with you to the funeral tomorrow. Then we must get back to Philadelphia."

Thelma brought tea and cookies. She was far from elegant as a maid, and rather unexpectedly offered her hand when Michelle introduced her.

"Please ta meetcha, I'm sure," Thelma responded with a grin. "I never knowed Michelle's mom, but I knowed you was relation the moment I seen you."

"We appreciate all you have done for Michelle," Grandpa said. "With your help, she has grown to be everything we expected, and more."

A moment of silence followed, until Thelma took the hint and left the room. Grandma turned to Michelle with a serious look on her face.

"Michelle, dear," she said. "We have come to talk to you about your future. It will be difficult for you, a young woman, to keep Plainfield Arabians going. To make a long story short, we would like you to live with us in Philadelphia. We will pay for your college education, and out East you will have opportunities that you do not have living in this little town in farm country."

Like many Easterners, Grandma thought that the vast spaces between the two coasts were a cultural wasteland, which produced needed crops and industrial products, but were no place for people with money to live.

Grandpa chimed in.

"Michelle," he said, "as long as your mother was alive, we subsidized Plainfield, which never made money. She loved it here, and we were willing to help her lead the kind of life she wanted. After she died, we refused to contribute money to your father, for reasons that I won't go into. We tried then to get custody of you, but failed. Now that your father is dead, and you are legally of age to make your own decisions, we want you to come live with us."

Michelle did not know how to respond to this surprising offer. At the moment, she was beaten down by the twin blows that had fallen on her. She had not thought about her future; she was struggling to get through each day. But deep down, she knew that she belonged at Plainfield with the horses.

While she hesitated, Grandpa said:

"We are staying in Chicago at the Palmer House. We will drive out for the funeral tomorrow. Please think it over."

Michelle quickly returned to her room, put on her denims, and gave her grandparents a quick tour of the farm. Grandma was mainly concerned with her white shoes, but Grandpa was game to see everything.

"Just like your mother," he said, proudly. "She loved horses, and all the work and muck that go with them!"

Then they said their farewells and returned to Chicago.

In the meantime, plans were being made for Dad's funeral. Since Michelle knew nothing about such matters, and was too distraught to do anything, Uncle Jim and Aunt Chloe informed Rev. Wiseman that they wished to have the funeral at the church. They asked the Dullard brothers, who operated the local funeral home, to make all necessary arrangements.

At that point Rex Montagu, a friend of Dad's, stepped in. Rex resembled Dad in many ways, with his lean muscular build, dark complexion, trim mustache, stylish clothes, and debonair manner. He owned a chain of men's clothing stores scattered in malls throughout the Chicago area. He was an expert rider and crack shot. He had met Dad at horse shows, and was a frequent visitor to Plainfield. During hunting season he often joined Dad and Uncle Jim hunting pheasants and ducks, which abounded in the low-lying land along the Kishwaukee River.

Rex had never met Mom, who had died earlier, but he had observed Michelle as she grew into a pretty teenager and talented rider and trainer of horses.

Rex turned up in his low-slung convertible as soon as he heard of Dad's death. He was aware that Dad had many friends among horse people and sportsmen throughout the Midwest and beyond. He was determined that his cosmopolitan friend would not suffer the indignity of a rural Illinois funeral. When he offered to attend to the details, Michelle was relieved. She was in no condition to meet large numbers of strangers, some from exotic backgrounds.

Without Rex, Michelle and the Dullard brothers would have been overwhelmed. An Arab sheik sent his regrets that he could not attend, but wanted his "good friend" to rest in comfort, and he volunteered to pay for the casket. Rex ordered a magnificent specimen, brought in from Chicago. Flowers and letters of condolence flowed in from many parts of the world; Rex took care of the acknowledgements. A famous tenor from the Lyric Opera volunteered to sing, and brought his personal accompanist with him. Rex enlisted formally dressed sales clerks from his stores to serve as ushers. He arranged for a caterer to serve food and drinks on the church lawn. The Dullard brothers were intimidated by his insistence and assurance, and Rev. Wiseman did not know what was happening until the day of the funeral.

Plainfield was a short drive on I-90 from O'Hare Field, and on the day of the funeral the two-lane state highway from the interstate to Clarksville was choked with big cars, some rented, some not. The First Lutheran Church was jammed to the rafters. Dad was well liked in the community and most of the residents turned out. The locals looked on with amazement as large numbers of well-dressed outsiders, with their bejeweled wives or girlfriends crowded the pews. The visitors revealed an aspect of Dad's life that few residents of Clarksville were aware of.

When the funeral took place, Michelle was too depressed to do more than go through the motions. Ever since Mom died, Dad had been the central figure in her life. She was just beginning to realize what his absence would mean. Her pain was eased to some extent by the presence of her grandparents, Uncle Jim and Aunt Chloe, and Clara and Rusty. After the service, Rex stood by her side, introducing her to the guests who had come from a distance. She was in a daze, responding mechanically with a handshake and "Thank you for coming."

Grandpa and Grandma stood aside, wondering who these people were.

"They look like they just came from the racetrack," Grandma said, lifting her eyebrows.

Politely, the locals waited their turn until the visitors had offered their condolences. Michelle came to life when family friends and local residents showed their affection for Dad with reminiscences that they wished to share.

In the meantime, the visitors turned the funeral into a party on the church lawn, greeting each other and conversing on familiar terms. Michelle realized that her father would have loved it, had he been alive to enjoy it. She felt grateful to Rex for relieving her of a responsibility that she could not have handled.

As the people were leaving, Grandpa and Grandma, who had been waiting patiently, stepped up to say "Good-bye" to Michelle.

"When you have had time to think about your future," Grandpa said, "please let us know. We want very much for you to come out East and live with us."

Michelle already knew her answer. She gave Grandma a hug, as tears began to flow. Grandpa's eyes were blinking as he held her close and kissed her on her forehead.

"Thanks so much," Michelle replied. "You are wonderful grandparents. I always enjoyed those visits to Philadelphia. I missed them when they stopped. I'll visit you, every year, and I hope you will come to Plainfield, too."

She managed a weak smile and said, firmly: "This is where I belong."

That evening Michelle walked down to the barn, where the horses were in their stalls. For the past several days they had heard the sounds of people coming and going. Michelle's visits had been irregular. They knew that something was amiss. They were relieved when Michelle appeared among them, calling them by name and stroking them. Fatima sensed her mistress' sorrow, and uttered low sounds of sympathy. Akbar, who assumed that some enemy was the cause of the trouble, was snorting and stamping, but Michelle's presence calmed him down a bit.

The familiar sights, sounds, and odors of the horses and the barn calmed Michelle's troubled soul. She returned to the house and slept well.

# CHAPTER 3

# *Lawyer Smart*

Plainfield Farm consisted of approximately ninety acres of rolling woodland and pasture along the Kishwaukee River, about eighty miles northwest of Chicago and a few miles south of I-90. Dad's grandfather, whose portrait hung in the hallway, had purchased the land and an adjacent farm during the Depression of the 1930s. He built the elegant white house with a broad veranda in imitation of his childhood home in the blue-grass country of Kentucky. Dad's father inherited both farms shortly after World War II. He converted Plainfield into a horse farm, and rented the other farm to a tenant to provide income to support his unprofitable Arabian horses.

In addition to the house, Plainfield was equipped with a commodious barn, which included an oval arena for exercising and showing the horses. Adjoining the barn was a spacious paddock, where the horses were kept when not in the barn or out to pasture. An additional feature was a quarter-mile track where the horses could get a good workout. There were sheds for hay, feed, and sawdust, which was used for bedding. The farm place was enclosed by a wooden post and rail fence. The house and buildings were painted white, with green trim. A working windmill that spilled cold, deep well water into a large stone trough announced the presence of the farm to travelers along County Road 7. A winding graveled drive led from the county road to the house.

In 1976 Dad inherited Plainfield. His elder brother, Jim, a working farmer, inherited the other farm. It seemed an unfair exchange, since Uncle Jim made a good living raising corn, hogs, and soybeans, but Dad was satisfied. As a boy, he was a charmer, who showed no interest in farming and was reluctant to perform any kind of manual work. He took a keen interest in horses and outdoor sports. He rode beautifully, and contributed to the growing reputation of Plainfield Arabians by exhibiting the family's horses at fairs and shows. When he married Mom he married money, which enabled him to maintain the farm and an elegant life-style.

Dad handled the business end of the farm, and traveled extensively to Europe and the Middle East. Mom took charge of the operations of the farm, working alongside her two employees, Luke and Ben. Luke was a local product, who began working part-time at the farm when he was in high school, and continued full-time after graduation. Luke was strong and capable, and operated all the machinery. He cleaned the barn, fed and watered the horses, disposed of the animal waste, and did almost everything that did not touch the bodies of the horses. Luke also tilled a field of about twenty acres where they grew alfalfa mixed with grass. He and his wife, Lena, lived in a small cottage near the windbreak of trees that outlined the farm place. Lena worked in the house as cook and laundress, and helped Luke with the chores in the barn.

Ben, an elderly black man, who had worked for Dad's father, was custodian of the equipment and the health and well being of the horses. He lived in a small apartment attached to the stables. Luke and Ben got Sundays off, but Ben rarely left the farm. Luke and Lena would visit her family on Sundays for church and dinner, but they usually returned about 4:00 p.m. to do the evening chores.

Mom's death complicated matters, but Michelle was able to pick up some of the slack. Like her mother, Michelle loved hard, sweaty, physical work, and welcomed the gratifying sense of exhaustion that came with a job well done. The work of caring for the horses was unending. Every morning, Luke fed and watered the horses, cleaned out the stalls, and laid down fresh bedding. Michelle cleaned, brushed, and saddled them. Ben walked the horses to give them gentle exercise before being ridden. Michelle gave them a good workout, riding them in the arena, or, in good weather, on the outside track. Then they were sent out to pasture.

The horses had to be fed, watered, and groomed again in the late afternoon, when they were returned to their stalls. Every evening, before going to bed, Michelle stopped in the stables, giving each horse some personal attention. Her hands were working hands: strong with tough skin. One reason for her superb figure was that her smooth back and shoulders and firm tummy were shaped by real muscle.

In the summer, Michelle had more time to work with the horses, especially the younger ones. Summer was the season for showing horses, taking them in trailers to gatherings of horse people. After Mom died, Michelle began traveling with her father. Her good looks, charm, and riding skills helped attract potential buyers.

The day after the funeral, Lawyer Smart (his real name) called and made an appointment to see Michelle in his office Thursday morning. He said it was urgent that he inform her of the status of her father's estate.

Lawyer Smart had been given his first name by his parents, who expected him (rightly, as it turned out) to go to law school and join his father's legal practice in Clarksville. He had served as the family attorney for Dad's father, and for Dad and Mom when they took over Plainfield Farm. He performed the same service for Uncle Jim. Waldo Smart was his son. Lawyer had hoped that Waldo would study law and join the practice, but Waldo had other interests. It seemed that the succession of Smart attorneys would come to a close.

Lawyer Smart was a tall, dignified, heavy-set man; in Victorian times he would have been called "weighty" for several reasons. His rich, deep voice had been cultivated in courtrooms, where he could usually convince a jury. Of course, he did not take any case if he did not think his client was in the right. He was a close friend of Rev. Wiseman and Dr. Carey. They provided a triumvirate of men of sense and community spirit who were sorely tried by their common nemesis, Bubba Grubbs, father of Sonny.

"Please sit down, Michelle," Lawyer said, although he remained standing. He moved slowly around the room, occasionally examining something on his desk or looking out the window, as if he were addressing a jury. In his early years Lawyer Smart had developed elements of showmanship, in the courtroom and in his office, which had served him well and had become part of his personality. This trait annoyed Mrs. Smart, who thought he overdid it in such mundane matters as carving the Thanksgiving turkey.

"Michelle," he began, "I have bad news for you. I'm afraid that your father was not a good businessman. Much as I enjoyed him as a friend and client, after your mother died I viewed with increasing dismay his financial improvidence. I did legal work for him, primarily concerned with the sale of horses. I was not directly involved in his business dealings, but I did participate in negotiating loans for him, and in some emergencies I put up my own collateral."

He paused to let his words sink in.

"I don't know anything about that," Michelle said, "it seemed to me that we were doing a good business with the Arabians. We always had plenty of money."

Lawyer Smart broke the bad news as gently as he could: "The brutal fact," he said, "is that Plainfield Arabians is bankrupt. I do not know how many unpaid bills are out there, but I suspect there are many, and for substantial amounts."

He dislodged an imaginary piece of lint from his lapel, and continued.

"Most of the earnings from the horses," Lawyer Smart explained, "went to your father's travel expenses, which I thought were much higher than necessary. Of course, he was moving among wealthy people, and he had to keep pace with them, to some degree."

Michelle was shocked by this unexpected news. In the past few days, one blow after another had fallen upon her, and she was unable to absorb this latest.

Lawyer Smart turned his broad back and looked out the window.

"That is not the worst," he said, still looking out the window. "Bubba Grubbs holds a mortgage for $240,000 on Plainfield Farm, including the house, land, and other buildings but not the horses, of course."

Michelle knew who Bubba Grubbs was, because he regularly attended football games and other athletic events, where Sonny starred. He screamed epithets at the officials when they called penalties or fouls on Sonny, a frequent occurrence given Sonny's reckless style of play. When Sonny made a good play, which also happened frequently, Bubba stood up and led the cheering. Mrs. Grubbs, a drab, beaten-down woman, sat silently. In fact, she was almost always silent anywhere she went, and to the people of Clarksville she was a mystery woman.

Lawyer Smart paused as he turned to face Michelle.

"Bubba never overlooked any possibility, no matter how remote, to turn a profit. The mortgage included an accelerated payment clause. It said that if your father died before the payments were completed, the mortgage was due and payable with 120 days. I pointed this out to your father and argued against it, but he refused to listen. Like any man his age, he did not expect to die. If the worst happened, he assumed that Plainfield would be sold and the mortgage paid off."

Michelle gasped. Her spunky nature, beaten down by one disaster after another, asserted itself.

"But I don't want to sell Plainfield," she said, firmly. "Plainfield is my life. I don't want to lose my Arabians. I won't do it, and nobody can make me do it!"

The fire in Michelle's eyes and the determination in her voice surprised lawyer Smart, but that did not change the realities of the situation.

He took another tack.

"I met your grandparents at the funeral," he said. "They are fine people. They want you to live with them. As your attorney and your friend, I must say that it would be best for you to face reality and accept the wonderful opportunities that they have offered you."

Michelle sat silently for several minutes. Tears began rolling down her cheeks, although no sound was heard. Lawyer Smart quickly took his neatly folded handkerchief out of his breast pocket and offered it to her. He had always liked Michelle, and even hoped that some day she would become his daughter-in-law.

"Michelle," he said, softly, "I see that you need time. I will help you buy some time in any way that I can. There are debts that need to be paid off immediately. Talk to Uncle Jim and Aunt Chloe; they own their farm free and clear. Perhaps they will provide temporary financing to enable you to clear the backlog and give you time to settle these matters to your satisfaction.

Jim has no interest in horses, and always thought that Plainfield Arabians was a mistake. The most you can expect is that he will provide a loan that will tide you over for a year or two."

Smart took a few moments to organize his thoughts.

"I can probably find lenders," he said, "who will give you a new mortgage to help you pay off Bubba. But the most I could expect to raise is about half the amount needed. Jim got the farmland, and Plainfield isn't good for much except raising horses or other livestock. Even with the new mortgage, you will have to raise $120,000 in cash to pay off the rest."

He bent over his desk and checked his desk calendar.

"You have 120 days," he said, "which means Monday, October 4."

He waited for Michelle to say something, but she sat silently. She was too depressed to think clearly.

"Under the circumstances," Smart continued, "the most reasonable course of action would be to sell Plainfield and the horses to some other horse breeder. That should enable you to pay off Bubba, with something left over to begin your life anew. That seems to have been what your father expected."

He helped Michelle to her feet as she prepared to leave. She felt dizzy as the extent of her financial predicament became clear. As she turned toward the door, Smart added:

"There are matters that concern you arising from the class party, but I need to talk to some people before making the next move."

Lawyer Smart had already consulted with Rev. Wiseman and Dr. Carey about bringing charges of sexual assault against Sonny. He had also called Charley Foxx, the state prosecutor for Kishwaukee County. In a small town like Clarksville, more often than not public business was settled by private conversation, rather than through bureaucratic channels.

Smart and Foxx were long-time friends and golfing partners. Foxx was especially responsive to Smart's call, since Sonny had already had some skirmishes with the law involving vandalism and disorderly conduct. Bubba had always been able to settle these matters by paying off the people who complained, but Foxx knew the signs of a young man heading for serious trouble. He wanted to intervene before it was too late.

Michelle stumbled out of Lawyer Smart's office in a daze, her eyes blinking in the bright sunlight. Slowly she drove home, hardly noticing where she was going. As she came up the drive, she saw the horses grazing peacefully in the north pasture. How she loved Plainfield and her life there! A deep sense of sorrow welled up from the depths of her soul as she contemplated losing it.

When she arrived at the farm, she recalled Rev. Wiseman's advice. She entered the house quietly and put on her jeans. She went down to the barn, where she put on her boots. Many of her usual chores had been left undone during the previous days, and she set to work with a will.

She cleaned and brushed each of the horses, who welcomed her attention. The work energized her and restored her sense of self-worth and physical well being. Then she saddled the horses and took each one for a good workout on the track. Events of the previous days had been highly unsettling, and the horses welcomed the confident touch of their mistress' hands and knees. Akbar was almost too overwrought, and Michelle had difficulty controlling him. She was well aware of the enormous power of the stallion, and she never forgot her mother's death. She knew that horses could respond suddenly to surprises, and that the rider had to be ready to react.

When she mounted Akbar, Michelle decided that it was best to give him his head and allow him to let off steam until he calmed down. She rode him out of the paddock and let him run in the pasture. He took off in a wild gallop, as Michelle struggled to bring him under control. Then the excited young stallion noticed a big Lincoln Town Car coming up the drive. As the car approached, Michelle saw that Sonny Grubbs was in the passenger seat, and Bubba was driving. Immediately she tensed up, and Akbar felt it. His warrior instincts kicked into action as he sensed an enemy. Suddenly he turned and headed for the car. At full speed he leaped the white wooden fence, with Michelle hanging on for dear life.

Sonny recognized the rider, and the car stopped. Akbar did not. When he reached the car he reared up on his hind legs, eyes blazing and nostrils flared, nearly throwing Michelle. He struck at the side window of the car with his powerful hooves. Michelle saw Sonny duck for cover. Bubba, his face purple with rage, opened the glove compartment to get what Michelle assumed was a pistol.

"Akbar, run!" she shouted as she jerked his head to the left and jolted him with her knees. "Run, Akbar, run!"

Akbar grasped the command: he raced full speed across the road, into the alfalfa field, and across the field toward the wooded stream where Mom had been killed when the horse she was riding had panicked.

"Akbar, Akbar," Michelle screamed, as she struggled to bring the mighty beast under control.

Suddenly Akbar swirled to head back to the car, throwing Michelle to the ground. Enraged, the stallion continued toward the car without his rider. By that time Bubba Grubbs had turned around in the gravel driveway and was high-tailing it back down the road. As the car left in a cloud of dust, Akbar reared again on his hind legs, waved his front hooves in the air, and uttered a cry of triumph. He had successfully driven off the enemy, and he had protected his mistress from those who would harm her.

As Michelle arose and dusted herself off, she realized that she had no broken bones, although she suspected that she would have aches and bruises by morning. Proudly Akbar trotted back to her, looking for signs of her approval. Michelle gave him the expected strokes, and attempted to remount. She could not. She was weak from her wild ride. Wearily she took the reins and walked back to the paddock with Akbar.

Akbar was still agitated, and his glands poured adrenalin and testosterone into his system. As the stallion continued waving his head, stamping the ground, and jerking the reins, Michelle got an idea. The other horses were in the paddock, but Sybil, Fatima's filly, was in heat and was confined to her stall. This would be the first time for Sybil, and Michelle had kept her inside because she wanted to wait for another cycle. Akbar was also young and inexperienced.

"What the heck," Michelle muttered. "Akbar did what he thought he had to do. He deserves a break."

With that she removed his bridle and saddle and took them into the barn. Then she brought Sybil into the paddock, leading her by her halter. Akbar looked around and spotted Sybil. His head went down as he approached the filly. Slowly the tube between his hindquarters began to grow. Sybil became aware of his threatening presence, and looked for her mother. Fatima, who had been through this process many times, turned her back and moved away, the other horses following.

Abandoned to the menacing stallion, Sybil trotted delicately toward the fence, where Michelle was waiting. Sybil was surprised as she felt strange and exciting sensations: anxiety was combined with anticipation. Akbar came closer, snorted, and nosed down her body. Sybil trotted away again, but not too fast and not too far. Akbar kept coming, as Michelle stood by the fence, watching a scene that she had seen many times before.

Michelle saw that Akbar was ready, and had had enough of this game of cat and mouse. She stepped over to Sybil and took the anxious filly by the halter. Sybil calmed down as Michelle stood by her side and stroked her neck. Akbar's tube was now extended full length in a gently curved arc, swaying from side to side and dripping at the tip. With a rush, Akbar leaped on Sybil's delicate back. When he had some difficulty connecting, Michelle deftly guided his tube into the target. A few snorts and grunts and the job was done.

Akbar pulled away, his tube still extended, but his agitation quieted. Sybil blinked and shook her head. As she trotted off to join Fatima and the other mares she looked startled but rather pleased.

Thelma, who had seen Michelle's wild ride and the attack on Bubba's car, called out: "Mickey, Mickey, are you O.K.?"

"I'm fine," Michelle replied. "Could you fix me a lemonade?"

# CHAPTER 4

# *Bubba Grubbs*

The next morning Michelle received an urgent call from Lawyer Smart. Bubba Grubbs, he said, had called his office and was furious at Akbar's attack on his car. Bubba threatened to prosecute Michelle for reckless endangerment and get the Animal Control Board to destroy the stallion as a threat to public safety. Worst of all, he demanded repayment of the mortgage within the contractual 120 days. In fact, Lawyer Smart said, Bubba was so furious that he was prepared to begin foreclosure procedures immediately, since Dad was four months behind in his payments.

As an attorney, Lawyer Smart's main activity was not winning cases in the courtroom, but straightening out problems before they reached that point. Years of experience had taught him that, no matter bad things might look, they often got worse. In short, he needed to see Michelle immediately.

Bubba had turned up in Clarksville a few years earlier, where he had established himself as a realtor. He seemed to have unlimited capital, and he soon drove the small-town realtors out of business. He built a development on the east side of town with big houses and a golf course. As high tech industry spread westward from Chicago along I-90, prosperous executives and professionals purchased his houses and townhouses.

The development brought franchised restaurants and motels with it, including an outlet mall. It was rumored that Wal-Mart was on the way. Some said that Bubba was trying to purchase the Clarksville National Bank and Trust, which would provide the last link in his control of the local economy. Others said that he wanted to open a casino. People appreciated the new jobs that Bubba had generated, even though most of them were low-paid. He had contrived to get himself elected chairman of the county board, where he controlled the sheriff, rural roads, and county zoning of unincorporated areas.

When Michelle entered Lawyer Smart's office, Bubba was there. He had calmed down considerably. Bubba expressed his regret at Dad's death, saying that he always enjoyed doing business with him. Michelle, of course, apologized for the attack on Bubba's car, explaining that her young stallion was impulsive and willful, and sometimes got out of control. She had no idea, she said, why he attacked Bubba's car, since he was accustomed to visitors. Lawyer Smart intervened to point out that the State Farm insurance office was just down the street, and they would take care of the damage.

At that point, they got down to business.

"Bubba," Lawyer Smart began, "Michelle knew nothing of the mortgage on Plainfield until yesterday morning. Plainfield has been her home since birth, and she is determined to keep it. She also wants to keep the horses, although she is now aware that the business in Arabian horses has not been profitable."

He paused a moment, as he adopted his usual courtroom manner.

"At present," he continued, in his mellifluous voice, "I am looking for financing to enable Michelle to repay the mortgage, or at least half of it within 120 days. I hope you will be willing to ignore the clause concerning her father's death, and permit the remaining $120,000 of the mortgage to run its normal course, unless Michelle can pay it off sooner. She needs time to decide what to do next. She can probably make the back payments in a week or two, and can be expected to make future monthly payments on time. She has other debts and expenses that will have to be dealt with immediately."

Bubba's response was surprisingly cordial.

"Don't yew worry yo' pretty little haid 'bout the cah," he said to Michelle. "The INsurance will take care 'a that."

Then he turned to Lawyer Smart. The low-level cunning that had made him successful in Clarksville was evident on his face.

"As to the mo'gage," Bubba continued, "Michelle is a fahne young gal—the prahde of Clahksville—and ah wish her the best. So does Sonny, if ah may say so mahse'f. Ah will settle fo' half in 120 days and continue the rest of the mo'gage if Michelle will pay up the arreahrs by the end of the month and remain current with future payments."

Bubba stood up, to indicate that in his mind the deal was settled.

Lawyer Smart looked at Michelle, who sat there with a surprised look and finally nodded agreement. Lawyer Smart was willing to accept the deal as the best that could be obtained. Bubba asked Smart to draw up the necessary papers, and arrange the financing to pay off half the mortgage by October 4. Then he asked Michelle if he could bring the papers out to Plainfield that afternoon to be signed. Michelle was relieved that she had been given breathing space, and agreed without thinking much about it.

Lawyer Smart immediately smelled a rat. He feared that Bubba was trying to cut a deal about Sonny's conduct at the party before charges could be brought. Reluctantly he agreed to the meeting:

"I see no problems," he said, "if your visit is limited to the financial arrangements that we have agreed to here."

As Michelle drove home, for the first time she had to face the real-world problems of money, or the lack of it. She had never thought much about money; her own needs were simple and inexpensive. She realized that her father had been under intense financial pressure. She had just learned that he had brought many of his problems on himself. She resolved that she would never make that mistake.

When Michelle returned home, Thelma was waiting for her on the veranda.

"Luke, Lena, and Ben are waiting to see you," Thelma said. "They are concerned about their future."

Luke knew that payments at the feed store were months in arrears. He had been told that after June 1 all purchases must be paid in cash. The farm had already used up its inventory and was feeding the horses with homegrown hay, without the oats, ground feed, and supplements that were necessary for health and vitality. The gas station where Rusty worked demanded cash for gasoline, and the farm storage tank would soon be empty. Luke, Lena, and Ben had not been paid their modest salaries for two months, and in the two months before that they had received only partial payment. The same applied to Thelma, who had not received the household money for June, and was required to pay cash for everything she bought at the store.

The three sat on the sofa in the living room as they told their story, respectfully and with obvious regret. They admired Dad and had worked for him for years at low pay, because they liked their life at Plainfield. They did not understand what had gone wrong after Mom died. Ben had no place to go; he had expected to live at Plainfield for the rest of his life. Luke and Lena could probably rent a house in town and find low-paid, menial jobs, but they were happy in their little cottage back among the pine trees. They needed to know what to expect.

Thelma sat off to the side. She considered herself "family," but now she shared their concern. She had a pretty good idea of what had gone wrong, but she kept that to herself.

Suddenly Michelle's chest felt as if a heavy weight had fallen on it. She had difficulty breathing, but then she righted herself. She saw that these good people depended on her—they were looking directly at her, anxiously, waiting for her answer. Out of her ancestry rose a powerful sense of responsibility and determination. She knew, deep down, that she had to rescue the sinking ship.

Michelle stood up, strong and straight, and her eyes narrowed as she said:

"I want everyone to stay. I want to stay. I am determined to find a way. I'll get some cash to pay the unpaid bills and tide us over for a while. Please stay with me for the next few months. At the end of that time we all stay or leave together."

As she looked at their faces, she saw complete confidence and trust. She was amazed.

"These good people have accepted me as the mistress of Plainfield," she told herself. "They trust me to provide for them. I must not let them down."

As the three left, she turned to Thelma.

"Thelma," she said, "you must help me. I must find some way to make money, lots of it and fast."

Thelma gave her a squeeze.

"I have an idea," she said, with a sly look. "Gimme a coupla days, and I may have something for you."

Surprisingly, Michelle found that her mood of despondency and sorrow had disappeared. She was filled with the optimism of youth. She had taken charge of her own life, and had assumed responsibility for the lives of others.

She went down to the stables to share her newfound self-confidence with the Arabians. Fatima sensed immediately that Michelle had now taken on the role of mistress, and nuzzled the girl's neck to show her acceptance. The other horses followed her example. Akbar was less willing to surrender his haughty autonomy to a female, but he too saw before him a young woman worthy of the role of "master." After shaking his head, stomping his feet, and shuffling in his stall, he bent his proud head and touched his nose to her outstretched hand as a gesture of fealty.

Michelle heard a car crunching on the drive. As she left the barn, she saw Bubba Grubbs standing on the veranda waiting for her. Bubba's usual bluster evaporated as he saw a beautiful, confident young woman striding toward him.

Michelle was now on her own turf, the dignified turf of Plainfield, and that gave her an advantage over a low-life like Bubba Grubbs.

She invited Bubba into the living room, where he sat uneasily on the sofa.

"What can I do for you?" she asked politely. "I thought we settled our business affairs this morning at Lawyer Smart's office. I am ready to sign the papers. I assure you that I will do all that is in my power to meet the payments that we agreed upon."

Bubba squirmed on the sofa as he gathered his thoughts. Growing up poor in the hardscrabble country of East Texas, he had imbibed a strong sense of social class and deference to one's betters. He had risen to wealth and power in Clarksville, and in business he enjoyed beating down and humiliating people—like Dad—who had superior social status. But this visit was not about business, and he could not overcome a gnawing sense of inferiority.

"Well, Miss," he said, "Ah know as how you and Sonny had a fallin' out at the pahty. He's pow'ful sorry about what he done. Ah hope you will forgive him."

Michelle made no response, since it was clear that Bubba had more to say.

"You see," Bubba continued, "since you and Sonny was boyfriend and girlfriend, I kinda hoped that y'all would get hitched some day and live at Plainfield."

Michelle looked on, incredulously, as the words tumbled out.

"Sonny could work with me in the real estate owffice, and make good money. You two could live at Plainfield and you could keep busy with yoah ho'ses. Then kids would come along an' they would keep you busy tew. If you was willin', I'd tear up that mo'gage, so as you kids don't start out in debt."

Michelle tried to catch her breath after this astonishing proposal. People who raise horses know that the main quality in a good horse is "heart," developed over generations of selective breeding. Michelle felt the heart in her chest beating fast, but more important was the hitherto untested "heart" lurking within her soul.

She rose to her feet, face flushed, quivering with anger.

"Do you think that I would ever marry Sonny?" she asked. "Do you know that he tried to rape me last Saturday at the party? Do you know how he pushed me around at school and treated me as his property?"

"Marry Sonny!" she exclaimed. "I'LL PUT HIM IN JAIL!"

Bubba wilted under this barrage. Yet he could not help but admire Michelle's bravado. He had watched *Gone with the Wind* many times, and Michelle looked to him like the reincarnation of Scarlett O'Hara.

As he shuffled out of the house, Michelle felt pangs of sympathy for Bubba. In a way, he had paid her a backhanded compliment. He wanted something more for his family than mere money. And that something included her. And Plainfield. After all, Dad had married for social status and money too. Michelle put that thought aside. She knew that there had to be a better way to save Plainfield than marriage to Sonny Grubbs.

That evening Lawyer Smart called. His usually calm, resonant voice was tense and agitated:

"Michelle," he asked, "whatever happened at your house this afternoon? Bubba Grubbs just called me, and he is furious."

"It had nothing to do with business," Michelle replied, coolly. "It was strictly personal."

"What do you mean, nothing to do with business?" Lawyer Smart replied. "It had everything to do with business. Bubba says the deal we agreed on this morning is off. He wants all his money in 120 days. I think I can find half of it, but you have 120 days to raise the rest. Bubba is looking for blood! You have acquired a bitter enemy, with the power to get even with you, and then some. Whatever may happen, have nothing more to do with Bubba Grubbs or Sonny."

"I don't intend to have anything to do with them—ever!" Michelle replied, her temper rising.

"As to Plainfield, I'll save Plainfield if I can, but not with the help of Bubba Grubbs."

"I don't know what kind of personal business Bubba had with you," Lawyer Smart replied. "If it's about the party, leave that to me. Whatever his personal business was, and however you responded, our problem now—your problem, really—is to raise another $120,000 in 120 days. That means by October 4."

Then he hung up.

Michelle laughed aloud, as a great sense of freedom swept over her. She had made the first big decision of her young life and had bet the ranch on it—sink or swim!

Saturday was the wedding day of Clara and Rusty. Clara had been excused from her usual Saturday half-day at the box factory, and Rusty's boss at the gas station gave him a paid holiday. Rev. Wiseman conducted the service in the small chapel, since the only guests were the couple's parents and immediate family. Michelle was maid of honor.

After the ceremony, the wedding party adjourned to the local Denny's restaurant for the wedding dinner. When they were finished, the happy couple went to Clara's house to pick up her personal belongings and take them to the small apartment that Rusty had rented. Michelle followed with her wedding present, a beautiful floor lamp that her mother had brought to Plainfield from Philadelphia. After extending her hand and best wishes to Rusty, and engaging in hugs and squeals with Clara, Michelle went home. Clara and Rusty went to bed together for the first time and discovered that all the equipment worked as it was supposed to. They enjoyed their eighteen-hour honeymoon very much.

The next morning Rusty returned to work at the gas station, and Clara went to the nearest Wal-Mart and Target to pick up things for the apartment. After that, they resumed their lives where they had left off, but now they were partners.

# CHAPTER 5

# Thelma

The next morning Thelma came into Michelle's bedroom to help her dress for church. She found her young mistress sitting on a chair, wearing her dressing gown, unbathed, uncombed, and unready to go any place.

"What's eatin' ya, Mickey?" Thelma said. "Time to get ready for church. You missed last Sunday, and that was O.K., but this time the Reverend will expect to see you there. You can sit with Clara."

Michelle did not reply. She was feeling a letdown after the euphoria of the day before. She was confident that Lawyer Smart and others would come up with $120,000 to refinance half the mortgage, but the rest was up to her. She had to come up with $120,000 in 120 days. The task seemed impossible.

Her immediate prospects were improved by the impending sale of three two-year old geldings, which would enable her to pay off the arrears on the mortgage, buy feed, gasoline, and groceries, and make a payment on the back salaries of her employees. Michelle hated to part with any of the horses, but she had grown up with the understanding that the horses were there to be sold. Fatima had been with them since Michelle was a baby, and was a fixture. She was now too old to be sold. Akbar, the young stallion, represented the future, as did Sybil. As to the others, Michelle felt better when she knew that they would be well treated, which was the case in this particular sale.

Thelma interrupted her thoughts with a suggestion that began with a question

"Mickey," she said, "everyone has to make use of their God-given talents and assets to get along in life. Just think a minute. What special talents and assets do you have?"

Michelle shook her head.

"I have no special talents; I have no advanced education; I have no job skills except looking after horses. In that regard, I already have a job, but it doesn't pay enough."

"You've overlooked one thing," Thelma replied. "Your good looks. They are money in the bank."

Michelle shook her head again.

"I had an offer last week for my looks," she said, "and I turned it down. It wasn't worth it."

"That's not what I mean," said Thelma. "Don't put your looks up for sale; put them up for viewing."

Then Thelma turned intense, as she approached Michelle closer.

"Long before I come to work here," she said, "I was the costume lady for the North Halsted Gentlemen's Club in Chicago. In them days they put on what they called burlesque. There I dressed lots of girls, some of them good-looking, some of them not so good-looking, but they all made money. Those girls worked hard, and too many of them used alcohol and drugs to make the job easier to take, but they all made money—lots of it!"

Michelle hardly knew what Thelma was talking about. She paid no attention to the world of public entertainment, and especially not a burlesque club that had closed years ago.

"Is that where the girls strut around on a stage and take off their clothes?" she asked.

"Exactly," Thelma replied, as she saw her beautiful fish nibble at the bait. "Egg-Zackly!"

"Mickey," she continued, "you've got the face for it, you've got the body for it, you've got the smile for it. All you need is the will, a little coaching, and a lucky break."

As Michelle pondered this startling possibility, Thelma moved in to clinch the deal.

"The headliner when the club closed," she said, "was a gal named Gloria Van Tassell. She had been a big star at the Rialto on S. Wabash, but was over the hill when I met her. I was her dresser. She is now comfortably well off and retired in Park Ridge. I called her last night. She'll come to Plainfield and learn you the moves."

Thelma was now under full steam.

"Believe me," Thelma said, rotating her shoulders and hips, "Gloria could wiggle her butt in a way that drove the guys mad—mad enough to throw hunnert dollar bills at her when she got down to the basics."

"Whadda ya say, Mickey? Why not give it a try?"

Michelle looked dubious.

"Look," Thelma continued, "it's easy."

With that she tiptoed daintily around the room, as if she were wearing six-inch heels. She followed with a few stiff bumps and grinds, and pretended to be removing her bra.

The scene was so ridiculous that she broke into laughter, and so did Michelle. They laughed so hysterically that Thelma rolled on the floor and Michelle collapsed on the bed.

When they had gotten that out of their systems, Thelma pulled herself together.

"That's the general idea," she said, before going into hysterics a second time.

"Well, O.K.," Michelle agreed. "Call Gloria and ask her to come out. I'll listen to what she has to say."

"I already done that," Thelma admitted. "She's coming here this afternoon."

"Now, let's get dressed, like a good girl."

"I have to go down to the stables first," Michelle replied. "Luke and Ben have the day off, and there's a lot to do. But I'll be back to shower and get dressed in two hours."

"I feel better already," she added, as she pulled on her jeans.

Gloria Van Tassell arrived promptly at 1:00 p.m. in a big 1979 Buick, driven by a modest little man whom she called Biff. Her overflowing figure was only partially concealed under a loose-fitting, flowery summer dress; with an effort one could imagine the well stacked and firmly packed young woman who had once dominated burlesque in Chicago. She swept into the house in a regal manner, while Biff made himself comfortable on the veranda and read the Sunday *Chicago Tribune*. Gloria greeted Thelma like a long-lost friend, while making it clear that she was the grand lady and Thelma the faithful retainer, a pose that Thelma did not mind in the least.

When she saw Michelle, Gloria stopped in her tracks.

"Oh m'Gawd," she exclaimed in a deep, gravelly voice, "I didn't know they made 'em like that any more!"

She circled around Michelle, like a lioness trying to decide which part of the carcass was the most delectable, and then she plopped her ample rear on the sofa.

"Honey," she said to Thelma, "this one's a natural. Unwrap her right away."

While Michelle looked on in some bewilderment, Thelma began taking off her clothes, right down to the buff.

"Don't feel uncomfortable, Honey," Gloria said. "You'll soon get used to taking your clothes off in public. Nothing to it, when you've got what you've got!"

Gloria's enthusiasm soared into the realms of hyperbole, as she declared that Michelle could be the greatest stripper since Gypsy Rose Lee. While Michelle slipped into a dressing gown that Thelma had thoughtfully provided, Gloria leaned back on the sofa and waxed philosophical.

"You should know," she declared, "that the art of the ecdysiast—stripper to you—is to arouse men to the point that they will willingly pay a ridiculous sum to see your body up close, and then be driven to throw more money on the stage."

She paused, waiting for her major premise to sink in. Then she went on to her minor premise.

"That's not too hard to do for any reasonably well-equipped female if she knows how to do it. It's all written in the male DNA."

Thelma had read something about DNA in the newspapers, but Michelle rarely read a newspaper, except for equestrian news.

Seeing that she had an uninformed audience, Gloria set forth on an extended exposition of her scientific theory.

"The male DNA," she announced, authoritatively, "was formed millions of years ago, in the primeval slime."

"A lot of that slime still sticks," Thelma remarked, sourly.

Gloria would not be interrupted.

"The DNA is the genetic code that controls life, from the beginning to the end."

"As anyone who knows men will agree," she continued, "the sole purpose of male DNA is to perpetuate itself in competition with all the other male DNA that is out there. When the male DNA finds an attractive female, it tries to connect. If it does, the DNA goes on to the next generation, and so on down to the present."

Having offered her major and minor premises, she offered her conclusion.

"That's the only reason the human race needs men. Otherwise, us women could get along without them very nicely."

Thelma nodded approval of this scientific proof of male vanity and self-centeredness, as if she needed any. At this point she interrupted.

"Where do women come into all of this?" she asked. "We're the ones who arouse 'em and have the kids."

"Women are written into the male DNA," Gloria replied. "The DNA knows it needs women to keep the chain going."

"The male human being doesn't know much about the female, but he knows that the youngest, most beautiful women, are most likely to have kids that will grow up and carry on his DNA. Beautiful, because female beauty is nothing more than the standard dimensions perfectly achieved. Young, because in early times women didn't live very long. They had to hang around long enough to get the kids to where they could shift for themselves."

Gloria was just getting warmed up.

"Male DNA likes a big butt," she said, "because there is plenty of room for the kid to be born. It likes big boobs because it thinks they will produce plenty of milk for the kid."

Michelle was listening intently to Gloria's flow of words.

"Hey, wait a minute," she interjected. "There are lots of women who don't have the standard dimensions. They find a man. Some of 'em aren't all that young, either."

Gloria had thought a lot about male behavior, and had concluded that only the genetic code could explain it.

"You gotta remember," she replied, "male DNA is looking for a female who will raise the kids too. That means more than just a great body. It means womanliness: intelligence, kindness, tenderness, a sense of responsibility. All those wonderful things that make us women SPECIAL! Deep in the genes of every man is printed the picture of the eternal woman—Mother Eve!"

"Any woman who understands male DNA," she concluded, triumphantly, "can get a man to pay for the privilege of seeing her naked and throwing money at her. We call it marriage."

"Jeez," Thelma commented, "if I'd 'a knowed about that DNA stuff, maybe I could 'a gotten some man to look at me."

Michelle was amazed. She knew all about the breeding and bloodlines of Arabian horses, of course, but somehow she thought people and horses were different.

"O.K.," Michelle said, "you may be right about male DNA, for all I know. But I need tons of those hundred dollar bills by October 4. How do I get the DNA to pay up?"

"Let me show you," Gloria replied, as she rose from the sofa. She gave her hind end a tantalizing wiggle.

"See that?" she asked. "The DNA likes a wiggle. Just like a fish coming after a worm on a hook."

She shook her shoulders and ample bosom.

"See that?" she asked. "The DNA likes tits. Goes back to infancy. The DNA is basically infantile, anyway."

At that point Gloria went into her full act. She walked gracefully on stage, holding her head high, showing a lordly disdain for her minions gathered at her feet.

Then she flashed a dazzling smile, letting them know that she was kidding, and was concerned only to give them pleasure.

With tantalizing twitches, like a fly-fisher stalking a trout, she pulled off an imaginary elbow-length glove. She tossed it aside, casually, as a sample of better things to come.

While Michelle watched intently, and Thelma grinned proudly, Gloria went through her entire routine, although she left her clothes on.

"Wow," Michelle gasped. "So that's how it's done. I can do that! When do I begin?"

"Not so fast, young lady," Thelma interjected. "We've got to design and sew a costume for you. I'll do the sewing. Then you have to learn your moves. Gloria will help with that. Then we have to find a place for you to work. After a few times, we'll know whether it will pay enough to be worth it. Remember, we need a thousand dollars a day for the next 120 days. We've got to make the big time—fast!—or forget it."

"That's why you've got to have a big time costume," Gloria said. "Most of these modern strippers dress like whores, and maybe some of them make their costumes do double duty in their off-hours. Then they go through crazy acrobatics, twisting and turning this way and that and climbing up and down a brass pole. If a girl has a figure like Michelle has, she shouldn't try to show it off by stretching it out of shape."

"I don't see Michelle that way at all," Gloria continued. "I don't see her as another sexy bimbo with a great body. There's plenty of them around. In the big time you've got to show something special."

She launched into an extended exposition of her concept.

"I see Michelle as the epitome of womanly elegance: the beautiful blonde in the TV commercial who stands outside the theatre with a handsome man while the attendant goes to fetch the Lincoln Town Car. These rich new professionals with their twelve hundred dollar suits don't want bimbos. They want a good-looking woman who will adorn their lifestyle—someone they can proudly show off at the country club and bring home to mother."

Her eyes gleamed with anticipation.

"When our young lady here comes out on that stage," she added, "they're gonna see the perfection of fresh young womanhood."

Gloria based Michelle's costume on the conventional little black cocktail dress, high-lighted by a fake diamond necklace and earrings. She included a black garter belt holding up filmy black stockings and the briefest of brief panties. Michelle did not need a bra, and Gloria didn't want one. Michelle was fairly tall, but Gloria included six-inch stilettos. It took several days of practice for Michelle to walk in them without falling. Gloria's props included a cheap white shawl from Target and a small table and chair from the dressing room to be put on stage in advance by an attendant.

Gloria had brought with her the Harry James recording of "I'm in the Mood for Love."

"When that brilliant trumpet sound of Harry James rings out," she said, "you're going to have everybody's attention. Nobody can ignore Harry James, my dear, but nobody!"

Then Gloria called out the moves that she wanted, and Michelle gave them a try.

"Step shyly to center stage (not too fast, Honey!)—you're in the spotlight—let 'em know you're in charge—give 'em a saucy toss of your head (flick your ponytail)—look 'em over and give 'em a warm smile (that's it!)—take off the shawl and put it on the chair (gracefully, Michelle, gracefully, don't just drop it like a wet dishrag)—take off the necklace and earrings and put them on the table (take your time! take your time!)—turn your back and wiggle out of your little black dress (give 'em plenty of wiggle, that's it!)—let it drop on the floor and step out of it (dainty steps, Honey, dainty, dainty, I know you're a farm girl but don't walk like one)—toss your ponytail again (that always gets 'em, the DNA was a horse before it was a human)—strut around the edge of the stage and wiggle your boobs (there ya go)—talk to the guys in front (don't worry, you'll think of something)—go back to the chair and take off your stockings (stretch and kick your legs! Legs, Honey, legs! The guys like long, slim legs and you've got 'em, baby!)—do another strut and toss the stockings to the lads (make 'em float, so you've got 'em stretching and fighting to catch 'em)—panties and garter belt off next—pick up your shawl—play matador in front of your crotch (don't let 'em see it right away)—toss the shawl and sashay off stage—give 'em a quick wiggle and last look as you leave (that's great Honey, great; you catch on fast)."

"The main thing, Honey," Gloria said when they had gone through the routine several times, "is to take your time. Make 'em wait. That's the way the great Gypsy Rose Lee did it. She was elegant; she was confident; she poked fun at what she was doing; she poked fun at the guys for coming to see what she was doing; and when she got to the main point she had them throwing hundred dollar bills and shouting for more."

Gloria came out to Plainfield again on Monday and Tuesday to polish Michelle's technique. Sometimes she wondered how the old style would go over in this world of instant gratification, where the young males want the strip but not the tease.

"Gypsy Rose Lee," she said, "always left something to the imagination."

After one of the rehearsals, Gloria commented:

"The basis of the strip-tease is the fact that the male DNA needs time to work. The erection can come fast, but all them juices and little sperms gotta be whipped into a frenzy, and that takes time. The sperms have a long way to swim to reach the egg, and it takes a good shove to get 'em there. That's why the bride makes the groom chase her around the bed a few times—or used to, anyway. The bride knows instinctively that the male DNA needs time. These young strippers have forgotten that elemental fact, but the male DNA never changes."

It turned out that Michelle, in addition to being beautiful, was naturally sexy. She had an easy grace that fitted the image of elegant femininity that Gloria was looking for. Without thinking about it, she gave a delightful charm to every move that Gloria taught her. Gloria compared Michelle to Gypsy Rose Lee, Margie Hart, and other great strippers of the 1940s and 1950s, some of whom were still going in the early 1960s.

"I learnt my trade by watchin' them gals work at the Rialto," she said.

"Of course," she added hastily, "I was very young in them days.—Very young."

After two days of practice, Gloria declared that Michelle was ready. Thelma had appointed herself Michelle's manager. She knew a place where her young, inexperienced stripper could have an unthreatening tryout for her first dip into the waters of commercial sex.

# CHAPTER 6

# *Amateur Night at Big Bill's*

Big Bill's bar and strip joint was located along the Rock River in a run-down part of Rockford, the second-largest city in Illinois. Big Bill had a stable of girls who performed regularly, although he did not pay them. They depended on tips from the customers, and, perhaps, other services that the customers might desire off the premises. Wednesday night was usually a slow night, and occasionally Bill livened the scene with Amateur Night, which the guys referred to as "cattle call."

Some of the performers were girls looking to turn pro; some were out on a lark, seeking to please a boyfriend or find one. Many of them were there just to earn some extra money. Some of the customers were considerate and appreciative; others took a cruel delight in embarrassing the performers.

Thelma knew that there was no time to waste, and she decided to put Michelle to the test with only two days' practice. She called Big Bill's and put Michelle on the list of amateur performers for Wednesday, labeling her "Michelle, the Belle of Clarksville." Gloria came along to observe, and Biff drove them in his big Buick.

It was a short drive to Rockford along I-90, although they had some difficulty in finding Big Bill's place of business. They arrived a little after seven; the show began at eight. During the drive, Michelle huddled in a corner of the back seat, running her moves through her mind, over and over. She said nothing during the trip and insisted that she was too nervous to eat when Biff stopped at Steak 'n Shake for steakburgers.

When Biff let them off at the front door, Michelle looked up and saw "Big Bill's" in blazing lights. A long line of males, mainly young, was waiting for the doors to open: some were professionals, just off work and wearing suits and ties; others wore leather jackets and caps with the bill turned to the back. There were a few smirking high school boys, and a few old baldies. Michelle saw no women at all. She wanted to go home, but Thelma was insistent.

"Look here, Mickey," Thelma said, "you're not here because you want to be. You're here to save Plainfield and your horses. Now get in there and knock 'em dead. I'll get you ready, and Gloria will sit out front and observe."

With that admonition, Thelma led Michelle to the back door and found the dressing room. The stage manager showed them a clipboard that listed "Michelle, the Belle of Clarksville" as No. 4. Michelle was the only girl who had a helper, which led to suspicious looks from some of the contestants, who feared that they would be competing with a pro. Michelle's friendly manner, and obvious unfamiliarity with her surroundings, put them at ease on that score. When they saw Michelle's costume, they suspected that she was some rich girl out slumming. As Thelma expertly applied makeup, they realized that they were out-matched, but most of them were there just for the fun of it, anyway.

Thelma glanced at the other girls and whispered to Michelle: "It'll be a cakewalk. None of 'em's got anything that you ain't got and a helluva lot better—excuse my French."

Michelle had never considered her body in a comparative light. She had seen plenty of girls' bodies in gym class and elsewhere, but it had never occurred to her to consider the body as anything but part of the total person. Cautiously she looked around and saw Thelma's point. Her confidence and enthusiasm for the task ahead began to rise.

The girl sitting next to her was a tall, slim dancer named Elena. She had a Latino costume, with a wide-brimmed sombrero and a flowing cape. Michelle liked her immediately. Elena said that she had studied ballet and tap since she was four, and was majoring in modern dance at Northern Illinois University, about thirty miles away. She wanted to be a chorus girl in musical shows, and had already tried out several times in Chicago, without success. She hoped that stripping would enable her to eat and pay the rent while she waited for her lucky break.

It was past eight o'clock and the guys were getting impatient. They had left the bar and the tables, and crowded around the stage to cheer on their favorite. As the crowd became more unruly, they began chanting: "Bring on the girls, bring on the girls, bring on the girls." At the other end of the dressing room, the stage manager, clipboard in hand, was talking to Girl No. 1, who was paralyzed with fright. She refused to go on stage, and the manager disgustedly called for Elena, who was Girl No. 2.

Elena took her place at the entrance behind the curtain. The speaker system began playing a Latino rock tune, and she stepped out confidently, moving gracefully across the stage, swirling her cape. Someone in the crowd called out: "Take it off," and others joined in the cry. Elena had not yet reached that point in her dance, and she continued to follow her plan. She threw her sombrero on the floor and shifted to a passionate, head-tossing, Mexican hat dance. "Take it off, take it off" rang through the crowd, as rambunctious young men, overstimulated by beer and testosterone, began shouting stronger words. Rattled, Elena threw off her cape, revealing a tall, lean, flat-chested dancer's body.

A groan came from the crowd followed by boos, as the lads made clear their disappointment with her mammaries. Shocked, Elena fled the stage in tears. Michelle attempted to comfort her, but the humiliation was too complete. Rushing past the disdainful glances of the other girls, all of whom were adequately endowed, Elena grabbed her things and hurried out the door, cape wrapped around her, leaving her sombrero behind and not bothering to change into her street clothes.

The stage manager, a rather prissy fellow, stepped on stage to quiet the crowd. He urged them, in a school-teacherly manner, to show consideration for the fine young ladies of the Rockford area who had volunteered to entertain them.

"We want tits, we want tits," they replied, as the stage manager frantically gestured for Girl No. 3.

She was a stocky barmaid from the truck stop-warehouse area near the junction of I-90 and I-39. She performed to Elvis Presley's recording of "Jailhouse Rock." Husky truck drivers, who were her regular customers, had come in considerable number to cheer her on. They made it clear to one and all that they wanted her treated with respect. Consequently, she was received with exaggerated encouragement as she traipsed clumsily around the stage, flinging off garments, one after another, with cheery abandon. She had no sense of timing and finished quickly, wiggling a big bum at the crowd as she ducked behind the curtain. She received a hearty round of applause for being a good sport.

The crowd was now becoming unhappy with Amateur Night, and did not hesitate to show it in various ways, the most disturbing being leaving the place. The manager feared a riot if their animal instincts were not satisfied quickly.

That left it up to Michelle, who was still sitting at her dressing table, mentally running through her moves. As "I'm in the Mood for Love" rang out, the crowd was silenced immediately by the glorious sound of Harry James' trumpet. The loudspeaker announced "Michelle, the Belle of Clarksville."

Michelle awoke with a start as Thelma poked her: "You're on, Mickey. Knock 'em dead!" With the spotlight off, the stage manager unobtrusively put the chair and table by the curtain, stage left. As Michelle hurried to the entrance, the other girls were congratulating the barmaid, now wrapped in a sheet, who was pleased and relieved that she had done it.

The music had stopped. By now the lads had imbibed more than a few large plastic cups of beer, and were getting restless. "I'm in the Mood for Love" began again. Once more the loudspeaker intoned: "Michelle, the Belle of Clarksville." Anxiously the stage manager motioned Michelle to get going.

As she stepped on stage, Michelle was blinded by the spotlight and stopped, like the proverbial deer in the headlights. When the lads saw her—tall, slim, golden ponytail, sleek little black dress, sparkling jewelry, black stockings, high heels, and smooth shoulders draped with a white shawl—they burst into spontaneous applause. Instantly they knew that Michelle was someone special. Someone to show off at the country club, or even take home to mother.

Michelle moved into her performance, tentatively at first but gradually gaining confidence. "The main thing, Honey," Gloria had said, "is to take your time. Make 'em wait." Since Michelle had to remember each move, she welcomed time to think. At first she saw nothing out front of her but a black hole, but as her eyes adjusted to the light, faces came into view—a throng of faces, watching intently, strangely silent.

The moves began to flow: step shyly to center stage, give 'em a good look, let 'em know you're in charge, saucy toss of the head, flick the ponytail, laugh, look 'em over, give 'em a warm smile, take off the shawl, put it on the chair, take off necklace and ear-rings, put them on the table, turn your back and wiggle out of your dress, step out of it, toss ponytail, walk along edge of stage and wiggle boobs, talk to guys in front, back to chair and take off stockings, show legs, toss stockings into crowd, panties and garter next, use shawl to matador crotch, toss shawl and sashay off, final wiggle.

While Michelle was concentrating on her moves, she was dimly aware that she could hear nothing but the music. As she left the stage, Big Bill's rocked with thunderous applause and cheers. "More, more," they cried, stamping their feet. "Do it again! Do it again!"

A cloud of money fell like green snow on the stage. Wrapped in a white terry-cloth robe with a hood, Michelle sat bowed over her dressing table, her head in her hands, emotionally exhausted. The other girls looked on in awe.

The stage manager hurried to Thelma. "They want her back, they want her back," he exclaimed. "Get her back out there. Put some clothes on her—not too much—and get her back out there. At least have her take a curtain call. Do something, or they'll tear this place apart." The crowd was still roaring. When Thelma asked Michelle to take a bow, she shook her head. She had nothing left.

Then Thelma remembered the money. She rushed out on to the stage, picking up money by the handful and putting it into her skirt. "Take it off," someone cried, and the crowd joined in: "Take it off, take it off." They laughed and shouted as Thelma, bending her stiff bones with some difficulty, scurried around the stage.

Defiantly, Thelma glared at the crowd, gave them the finger, and performed an awkward bump and grind. That did it! Pandemonium! More money fluttered on to the stage.

The stage manager rushed out from behind the curtain.

"Get out of here," he hissed, as he tugged at Thelma's arm.

The crowd was having too much fun. They booed and shouted at the manager, and began throwing beer cups at him, some of them far from empty. Thelma and the manager fled, Thelma clutching tightly the money in her skirt. Fights broke out, and the bouncers tried in vain to maintain order. Sirens were heard, as the police arrived. The older men and suit-and-tie professionals hurried to the exits, while the guys with leather jackets and backward caps stayed to tangle with the cops.

Back in the dressing room Thelma stuffed the money into a satchel and poked Michelle, who sat in a trance at her dressing table, still wearing her terry-cloth robe.

"C'mon, Mickey," Thelma said, "we gotta get outta here." She gathered up Michelle's clothes, the costume, and the satchel. She grabbed Michelle's hand, and they headed for the back exit. The other girls were furious because they had missed their opportunity to perform. They shouted at Michelle and hit her with handbags, cosmetic cases, and whatever else was available.

Big Bill came in, looking frantically for Michelle.

"Where's dat kid?" he shouted. "I wan'er back tamarra. Who da hell is she, anyway?"

"She's the Belle of Clarksville," Thelma said as she pushed Michelle out the back door. "The stage manager has her number. Call me in the morning."

Gloria was waiting in the back alley, and Biff was there with the car. Thelma shoved Michelle into the back seat, and jumped in back with her. Gloria got in the passenger seat, and Biff drove off, pushing his way through the crowd, which was now standing on the sidewalk and in the street. The flashing lights of police cars illuminated the scene, but the police were relaxing, satisfied that the ruckus was over.

Gloria was ecstatic.

"You were great, Honey," she chortled. "Just great. I knew you'd be great. I just knew it!"

"And that pause," she added, "when you first stepped on stage, looking anxious and vulnerable—that was a stroke of genius."

"No stroke of genius," Michelle said wearily, leaning her head back on the soft Buick upholstery. "The spotlight blinded me for a moment—that's all it was."

"Whatever," Gloria replied. "It's going into your moves from now on. Do you know what those guys saw when you stood there? They saw virginity, that's what they saw: pure, dewy-fresh virginity. They saw the virgin bride, quivering with anxiety and anticipation, waiting for her eager bridegroom to take her in his arms—for bridegroom read each guy there."

Gloria rattled on, as Biff drove, Thelma counted the money, and Michelle slumped in her corner of the back seat, still wrapped in her terry-cloth robe.

"Guys have a great desire for virginity in their women," Gloria said, "although not for themselves, of course. It's the DNA. When the DNA sends them little sperms up the tube, it wants 'em to have a clear field and keep the guy's DNA chain going. They don't want some other guy's DNA slipping in ahead of 'em."

Michelle tilted her head back, and relaxed on the soft cushions of Biff's big Buick. Soon the quiet hum of the motor and the gentle motion of the car lulled her to sleep. Thelma finished counting the money: $485—not enough, but a good start. And she knew that Big Bill would call in the morning.

# CHAPTER 7

# *Marcella, the Belle of Carpentersville*

When Michelle came down to breakfast the next morning, she felt tired and vaguely uneasy about her strip tease the night before. Thelma was at the dining room table, which was covered with neatly stacked bills of various denominations, including a significant pile of fifties.

"Look at that, Mickey," Thelma gloated, "no hunnerts yet, but they'll be along soon. I'm waiting for a call from Big Bill. Gloria and Biff stayed here overnight, 'cause Gloria wants to work on the fine points and go back with us tonight. Get yourself in the mood for another trip to Rockford. And I'd like to have you take this money to the bank. I don't want it lying around here."

"First I've got to go down to the barn and take care of the horses," Michelle replied. "I may have turned into a glamour girl last night, but when I woke up this morning I was still a working girl."

The horses sensed a new sparkle in Michelle as she took care of her daily tasks. Showing off her charms to the boys at Big Bill's had awakened the sexiness in Michelle that had been latent during her schoolgirl days. There was a glint in her eyes that had not been there before. The horses felt it in her strokes as she cleaned and brushed them. They responded to her energy and flair as she took them through the usual morning workout. Fatima, the wisest of them all, suspected what it was.

Michelle had finished and was walking back to the house, when she saw an unfamiliar car coming up the drive. It stopped in front of the house and a man got out whom she vaguely recognized. He was Charley Foxx, the state's attorney for Kishwaukee County. He always wore a hat similar to the fedoras worn by men in the old black and white movies. He walked up to Michelle, extended his hand, and introduced himself.

"Michelle," he asked, "can I talk to you for a few minutes?"

Michelle guessed what Foxx had in mind, and found it difficult to breathe. She knew his visit must concern the party at the lake. She had done her best to forget it, but she was still haunted by nightmares in which Sonny's image, distorted into the form of an angry stallion, leered and came at her. The last thing that she wanted was to tear open the wounds that were just beginning to heal.

"Look," she said, testily. "If you want to talk about what I think you want to talk about, I have nothing to say."

Foxx was not surprised by Michelle's angry reaction. Victims of rape frequently take refuge in denial. A career in law enforcement had taught him the importance of timing, and he could tell by the look in Michelle's eyes and the tone of her answer that the timing was not right.

"Yes, Michelle," he continued, "I do want to talk to you about the party at the lake. It is possible that a serious crime was committed against you. I have already talked to Clara and Rusty, who told me what they know. I hope that some day soon—if not today—that you will help me decide what to do."

"Aha!" Michelle replied, angry and defensive. "You've already been talking to people about me. What happened at the party is my business, and I don't want to talk about it—to you or anybody."

She broke into tears and hurried into the house, leaving Foxx standing at the gate.

Foxx's career in law enforcement had also taught him the value of patience and persistence. He was willing to wait. He had planted an idea in Michelle's mind, and he hoped that it would eventually produce the result he wanted.

Michelle dried her tears, showered, dressed, and prepared to drive into town to deposit the money. She was far from comfortable with her involvement at Big Bill's. After stopping at the bank, she decided to pay a call on Rev. Wiseman. The good pastor also wanted to see Michelle, because he had been in touch with Lawyer Smart concerning Sonny Grubbs. Smart told him that the prosecutor was willing to bring charges of sexual assault against Sonny if there were credible witnesses.

The key witness would be Michelle, and Rev. Wiseman had agreed to ask her whether she would do it. Victims of rape often are reluctant to appear in court, because their humiliation will become a matter of public scrutiny. An unscrupulous defense attorney might try to get his client off the hook by attacking the character of the victim.

When Michelle appeared at his office door, Rev. Wiseman realized that something else was bothering her. He decided not to mention Sonny. Instead, Michelle told him about the possibility of losing Plainfield, which he already knew, because he was working with Lawyer Smart to find investors for a new mortgage.

"You have many friends, my dear," he said, "who will help you as much as they can. You will have to find the courage and determination to do your part. You should know that our hopes and prayers are with you."

Rev. Wiseman waited patiently for Michelle to respond. She hesitated for a long time. She was too embarrassed to speak. Suddenly she blurted out:

"I am told that the best way to make the money I need is to dance in a strip club."

She covered her face with her hands, shocked at what she had just said.

Rev. Wiseman realized that Michelle's only asset was her beauty. He was not a prude. As a young man in the army, he had gone with his buddies to the Folies Bèrgeres in Paris, which was artistic, as well as sexy. But now he was an ordained minister, and he was counseling a member of his parish. Lutherans are conservative people, and Rev. Wiseman was understandably startled when Michelle told him what she had in mind.

Having taken the leap, Michelle continued more confidently.

"The only way I can raise enough money to keep the farm and the horses," she continued, "is to become a stripper. Otherwise I will have to sell out, lock, stock, and barrel, and leave town."

Wiseman knew the family well. Michelle's mother had been a stalwart of the congregation, and had discussed with him at various times her marital problems with her unfaithful husband. The Reverend had baptized and confirmed Michelle, and had watched her grow up to be a beautiful and responsible young woman. He was far from keen on the idea, but he respected Michelle's determination to manage her own life. He felt confident that she would always try to do the right thing.

Faced with an unusual problem, Rev. Wiseman racked his brain to think of women in the Bible whose beauty had been used by God to achieve His purposes. One such woman was Ruth, whose charms caught the eye of Boaz while gleaning in the fields; she became an ancestor of King David and Jesus. Bathsheba's nude bathing stirred the loins of King David, and in so doing she became the mother of Solomon, wisest and wealthiest of the Israelite kings and builder of the temple in Jerusalem. The beautiful Jewish girl, Esther, won a beauty contest that was conducted to find a bride for the King of Persia, and in that way was able to help her people.

Considering Michelle's purpose, and the financial straits that she was in, Rev. Wiseman reluctantly decided to give her his acquiescence, if not his blessing.

"Your beautiful body," he said, "is a gift of God to be used for living. If you use it to save Plainfield and your beloved Arabians from the greedy grasp of Bubba Grubbs, you are, in my opinion, acting out of love. Remember, the disciple whom Jesus loved wrote: 'God is love.' God will understand."

Nevertheless, he warned Michelle that her new career would bring many temptations with it. "The most beguiling," he said, "will be to like the money and the attention so much that you won't want to give it up."

"Don't use your body for momentary gratification or selfish gain," he added. "It is an instrument tuned by its Maker to play the melody of love. When the right man comes along, your body will sing."

As she drove home, Michelle was considerably relieved by those welcome words. When she arrived, she found Thelma on the phone with Big Bill.

"Listen up," Thelma said, "you let people watch your floozies free of charge, just to sell beer. We'll come if you charge $10 admission, and we get the money. We keep the tips, too. You'll pack the place and sell more beer, and Michelle won't cost you anything."

Apparently Big Bill was willing to agree to Thelma's terms, because she asked him how many people the fire marshal permitted in the building. When he replied, she proposed at least twenty more, and hung up.

"Well, Mickey," she said, "Big Bill wants us for three nights—Thursday, Friday, and Saturday—and we get the ticket money. He'll squeeze 180 in that place, or my name ain't Marilyn Monroe. That's $1,800 or more per night for three nights, plus tips. You do two performances: 7:00 and 9:00. He wanted a performance at 11:00, but I told him you're a farm girl—which is true—and have to get up early to milk the cows, slop the hogs, and feed the chickens. For three nights we're lookin' at fifty-four hunnert in ticket money, plus at least half that much in tips. Mickey, we're going to make our $7,000 for the first week."

Michelle began to think that this crazy scheme might work. She remarked that there was a big backlog of chores to do in the barn, and it was time for her to put on her denims and get at it.

"Just one more thing," Thelma called after her. "The Rockford *Register-Star* learned about the fracas at Big Bill's from the police, and sent a cub reporter out there to find out what had happened. A few of the guys were still hanging around. They couldn't remember your name, but they thought it was Marcella and you were from Carpentersville. Big Bill is putting out posters and radio ads under that name. He wants to keep you under wraps—well, not exactly, considering what you will be doing—but to keep you away from the competition."

Thelma added: "Bill don't want no more trouble. He's hired four off-duty policemen to stand in front of the stage, plus his usual bouncers, and a squad car of cops will be nearby. Sounds good to me."

Biff drove into town and came back with a copy of the *Register-Star*. On p. 3 was a story headlined FRACAS AT AMATEUR NIGHT. The story stated that a strikingly beautiful contestant, believed to go by the name Marcella, the Belle of Carpentersville, had set off a fight at Big Bill's. Bill was quoted as saying that he expected the young lady in question to return tonight. Later Gloria learned that the story had been on local TV news, which offered a reward to anyone who could give information about the mystery girl.

With all this hype going on, Thelma looked forward to another big haul, as they returned to Rockford in Biff's Buick. Michelle was feeling good too, and ate a hearty steak for dinner, her first good meal since the graduation. A huge crowd was waiting for the door to open as they approached. A giant poster with a picture of a voluptuous blonde in a black evening gown advertised the return appearance of Marcella, the Belle of Carpentersville. Gloria knocked at the front door and was admitted. She took her place at the box-office, to make sure that she got all the admission money. Biff parked in the back alley, while Michelle and Thelma went in the back door.

This time Michelle had a separate dressing room with a gold star on the door. The other girls, who performed regularly at Bill's, gave Michelle sidewise looks, but made no effort to be friendly. Three girls would perform first, to warm up the crowd, and then Michelle's turn would come.

As Michelle heard the music playing and the girls coming and going, she began feeling butterflies in her tummy. She intended to begin with the deer-in-the headlight gimmick, and she had a feeling that it would come naturally.

The stage manager knocked at her door. She heard Harry James playing "I'm in the Mood for Love." The loudspeaker announced the feature attraction: "Marcella, the Belle of Carpentersville." When Michelle stepped into the blinding beams of the spotlight, she blinked and did the deer bit instinctively. The crowd had been waiting for her, and broke into cheers and applause.

At that moment Michelle felt wonderfully calm and confident: step shyly to center stage, give 'em a good look, let 'em know you're in charge, saucy toss of the head, flick the ponytail, laugh, look 'em over—Michelle froze. She thought she would faint. In the front row was Sonny Grubbs with Squirt Peterson and several of his buddies.

"Take it off, you bitch," Sonny shouted, "Take it off or I'll take it off for you." Squirt and the others joined in.

Obviously, Sonny was drunk. Michelle was too startled to run. Sonny leaped on to the stage, grabbed her, and began ripping at her dress, trying to get at her breasts. His buddies joined him. Thelma rushed in to help Michelle, but the off-duty police officers got there first. They pulled Sonny away from Michelle and handcuffed him. Then they started on his comrades, who had not expected to meet resistance.

The crowd enjoyed a fight almost as much as a pretty girl, and began cheering the combatants. Some jumped on stage to help the police; in the confusion they attacked each other, and fists began flying. Sirens were heard as the uniformed police appeared. Michelle managed to escape to the security of her dressing room, where she sat sobbing and trembling, wrapped in her terrycloth robe.

"I'll get you out of here, Mickey," Thelma said. She grabbed her by the wrist and led her out the back door, where Gloria and Biff were waiting. Prudently, Gloria had taken the ticket money with her, which totaled $1,800, although there would be no tips. Michelle noticed a strained look on the faces of Gloria and Biff, who pointed surreptitiously toward the car. As they approached, a dark, trimly built young man stepped out of the front seat.

"Get in da cah," he said, with a quick motion of his hand. "I'm not gonna hurt you. I'm here to talk business."

Biff got behind the wheel, Michelle and Thelma in the back seat, and Gloria in front. The young man squeezed in beside Gloria.

"Go down da street 'till I tell you to stop," he said. They had gone several blocks when he directed them into the shadowy parking lot of a hardware store that was closed.

"I am Ricky Marino," he said. "My fodder is Tony Marino."

Gloria recognized the name. Tony Marino was the vice lord of the western suburbs, with a nightclub in Rosemont called the Purple Orchid. She relaxed, confident that they were not the victims of a holdup.

"He's O.K.," she said, "I knew his old man, once, a long time ago."

"News in dis business travels fast," Ricky said. "I came out here to dis dump to scout. I liked what I saw, as long as it lasted. I am auttorized to make an offer on da spot, and dat is what I'm gonna do—right now."

The gist of his offer was that the Blue Orchid needed a sure draw, right away. Their top girl had quit, and there were several monster conventions in town, loaded with big spenders. Rosemont was adjacent to O'Hare Field, and the travelers would be staying in nearby motels, with time and money to spend. The Cubs were playing too, he added, with a snigger, which meant a lot of frustrated fans looking for action. He chuckled at his little joke, and even Biff, a White Sox fan, managed a wan smile.

Tony Marino wanted Michelle tomorrow night, Ricky said. He would pay $5,000 a night for two performances on Friday and Saturday nights. The patrons of the Blue Orchid did nothing so vulgar as throw money on the stage, but Tony's boys would circulate discreetly and collect tips placed in envelopes.

"We have poker in the back," Ricky said. "I have seen a big winner unload ten grand on a girl he liked."

"We are promised to Big Bill this weekend," Michelle said from the back. "Maybe next weekend."

"Fuck Big Bill," Ricky snarled. "Big Bill won't do nuttin'. Dat's my offer. And Tony Marino don't take 'no' for an answer."

Thelma said that they needed to think it over. She promised to call him first thing in the morning.

"O.K.," Ricky said, "I hope you know what's good for you."

He stepped into his car, which was parked in the shadows, and left.

As Biff drove home, Ricky's offer overshadowed the fracas that they had left behind. Michelle had never been to a place like the Purple Orchid, and the thought made her feel uncomfortable, but she would go along with whatever Thelma and Gloria decided. They, of course, were familiar with working for the mob, and felt no anxiety.

"They always pay," Gloria said, "and they won't touch you if you don't want it. They have wives and in-laws to keep them on the straight and narrow. That Ricky don't wear a wedding ring; he could be a problem. But Tony and I were once close—very close, you might say—and I think I can handle his kid."

Thelma chimed in.

"We're looking at $10,000 plus tips. This could be a great week. I don't know what to expect next—maybe they'll keep Michelle on at the Purple Orchid. Frankly, I think this is the break we've been lookin' for."

By this time Michelle was asleep in the back seat. Stripping had proven to be more strenuous than she had imagined. That night she bad dreams about Sonny; she had almost gotten over the rape, but now it all came back again.

The next morning Biff got a copy of the Rockford newspaper. A front-page headline screamed: MYSTERY GIRL STRIKES AGAIN. The paper speculated on the belligerence that Marcella seemed to evoke in those who watched her. Big Bill, who had already heard from Tony Marino, declared self-righteously that she would never come back to his place. Charley Foxx called the Rockford authorities and asked them to hold Sonny as long as possible, since Kishwaukee County might have charges more serious than disorderly conduct. Tony Marino put an ad in the Chicago *Sun-Times* that the mysterious Marcella would appear that night at the Purple Orchid. The *Chicago Tribune*, a more sedate paper, had a brief notice in its gossip column.

As she gave the horses their morning workouts, Michelle was oblivious to the excitement swirling around her. She was relieved to know that Sonny was in jail, at least for a while.

# CHAPTER 8

# *The Purple Orchid*

Michelle was astonished when she first saw the Purple Orchid, with its lavish decor, tiny tables with white tablecloths, and larger tables on the periphery. It was laid out on two levels, with a bar on each level, and a small stage raised to a medium height between the two. The club featured a cabaret singer named Zane—a tall, graceful black woman in her thirties, who was accompanied by a pianist. There was a small band for dancing and the strippers. Michelle's weekend trial proved successful, and Tony took her on permanently. She worked six nights a week at $10,000 per week, plus tips. She usually performed at 9:00 and 11:00, late hours indeed for a country girl.

It was an easy commute on I-90 from Plainfield to Rosemont, and Michelle continued to live at home, where she could work daily with the horses. Gloria and Biff settled in at Plainfield until Oct. 4. Gloria had been raised on a farm in Iowa and was not afraid to get her boots muddy, although she knew nothing about horses and had never ridden one. She took over many of the routine chores, while Michelle gave the horses their daily workouts on the track. Hard work made a noticeable improvement in Gloria's figure, although she complained that her hands were a mess.

Each afternoon, Biff drove Michelle to the club in his Buick, where he let her off and went to Gloria's apartment in Park Ridge, not far away. There he watched TV and read the newspapers. He came back to the club about midnight to pick up Michelle and drive her home. By that time she was tired, and fell asleep almost instantly in the back seat.

Michelle enjoyed those rides back and forth in Biff's big, powerful, soft-springed, heavily-upholstered Buick. She often wondered what he got out of reading the newspapers. The only opinion she ever heard him express was his disgust that the Cubs had installed lights at Wrigley Field.

"They said they needed them for the World Series," he muttered. "Ha! That'll be the day!"

One of the perks of the Purple Orchid was that the employees could order food from the menu, which would be delivered to a small alcove near the dressing rooms. Michelle tried everything and learned to enjoy a variety of foods, although the menu was mainly Italian, which itself has many varieties. At Plainfield, Lena had always served basic farm food: bacon and eggs or pancakes for breakfast, dinner at noon with meat and potatoes, garden vegetables, and a heavy dessert, and a light supper. As a growing girl, Michelle always drank milk with her meals. That changed when she began eating dinner at the Purple Orchid. Since she still lived at home and slept late, she asked Lena to prepare a kind of brunch for her about 11:00, and that satisfied her needs until dinner at the club. Michelle did not drink beer or wine, but for dinner she graduated from milk to Diet Pepsi.

Michelle had now perfected her performance. She enjoyed the sense of power that she felt on stage, when all eyes were fastened on her. As her sexiness asserted itself, she added some moves that Rev. Wiseman certainly would not have approved of. She wasn't sure that Gloria would approve of them either, but they drew a warm response from the customers, whose appreciation was best expressed in the little white envelopes.

All the strippers had beautiful bodies, of course, but Michelle revealed surprising talent as an entertainer, which added to her youthful charm. She used light-hearted nods and winks, intriguing raised eyebrows, comical shrugs and grins, and cute little giggles to communicate a sense of fun. Sometimes she used playful gestures with her hands and shoulders, or saucy bumps with her hind end, to punctuate her routine.

She remembered Gloria's advice ("take your time! take your time!"), and the removal of each item in her costume became a tantalizing little drama in itself. Always there was her dazzling smile. It was almost an anti-climax when her nude body finally gleamed in the spotlight.

At the Purple Orchid, Michelle had reached the big time. Most of the customers were high income young professionals, or affluent couples in their forties and fifties. Well-dressed elderly couples were not uncommon. Michelle delighted the women and aroused the men. The womanliness that Gloria had noticed began to show itself, and her attractiveness went well beyond mere sexuality. She became a fixture at the Purple Orchid, and the money piled up. Saving $120,000 by Oct. 4 was now a distinct possibility.

Michelle did not associate much with the other strippers, who were all experienced professionals. They resented her youthful beauty, and laughed at her naiveté. Her best friend was Zane, the singer. Zane was a river black from Memphis, born in New Orleans. She called herself "Miss Diversity" and compared her ancestry to Tiger Woods—a mixture of many races, with African-American predominating.

Zane was given her "zany" first name by her father, a jazz musician who loved the Western novels of Zane Grey. Her father's claim to fame was that he had been a sideman to Elvis Presley before Elvis became famous.

"He thought Elvis wasn't much of a guitar player," Zane laughed, "or much of a singer, either."

"But he recognized that Elvis was a great entertainer."

Zane was an avid reader, which helped fill in the time between performances. She read a dozen or more books a month, most of them paperback western novels by Louis L'Amour or romance novels by Jude Devereaux and other romance writers. Some of the books she read were of good quality. Michelle had never been much interested in reading—she was an active rather than a contemplative person. When Zane gave her a copy of *Lord of the Flies* she was fascinated.

Several times, Michelle invited Zane to Plainfield, where they enjoyed riding horses together, and went kayaking in the river. Zane joked that the air was too fresh for her, especially one time when they encountered Luke spreading manure on the pasture.

As she displayed her charms to others, Michelle became increasingly aware of her own sexuality. The voluptuousness and sensual movements of the strip tease stimulated her desire for the real thing. When she confided her feelings to Zane, her friend replied:

"If you go through the motions, you will feel the e-motions. No gettin' around that! Sometimes, when I was strippin', I would see a man out there, obviously interested, and gettin' a bulge in his pants. When that happened, I would get so hot I could hardly stand it."

"That's when I took up singing. At this time in my life, I don't want no more hot pants involvements. The price you pay is too high."

Zane took Michelle under her wing when she discovered that Michelle was a virgin. Zane's street smarts and no-nonsense trash talk were needed, because

Ricky, attracted to Michelle's blonde beauty, began taking an unwelcome personal interest in her.

Michelle talked to Zane about her problem: "That Ricky is hitting on me all the time," she said. "I've got to get out of here. Except I need the money I can earn between now and October 4."

"What's with October 4," Zane asked.

"Just that I need $120,000 to pay off half the mortgage, or I lose Plainfield, the horses, everything," Michelle replied.

"Plainfield is my life," she added morosely. "Without Plainfield I don't know what I would do."

"O.K.," Zane responded. "I want to get out of here, too. I used to work for Elite Escorts in Chicago. They aren't what you might think. They are really on the up-and-up, strictly no-touch, at least as far as the clients are concerned. The girls can touch the clients all they want."

Michelle had never heard of escort services or their reputation as a cover for prostitution.

"What's an escort service?" she asked. "Is that where you take people around town, showing them the sights?"

"You show 'em the sights, all right," Zane replied. "Elite Escort services is for very rich men, some of them homosexuals, who need a good-looking woman on their arm for business conferences, parties, and sometimes high stakes bridge or poker. To them, $5,000 is like five cents to you and me. The pay is terrific, but if you think Ricky is a pest, wait 'till you meet some of those guys. They think they are God's gift to women, and that they own you, body and soul, for an evening."

She threw her hands up in despair.

"I always got Nigerian diplomats or Arab sheiks," she complained, "some foreigner of color. I longed so much for an American that I was willing to give my services for free."

"Which I did," she added, "and enjoyed it very much. I even got one who read books! Afterward, he paid me anyway."

Michelle was game to try it, especially since Zane said she could work three nights a week and make as much as six nights at the Purple Orchid.

"There's one problem," Zane said, "Tony don't take kindly to girls who leave him. The girl whose job you got, lost her temper and left after a tantrum. She'll never work again—in a job that requires a pretty face. Ricky takes care of that sort of thing. I hate to think what he might do to you, especially since he wants you so bad."

Michelle thought again. She remembered that Gloria had remarked about knowing Tony Marino. She decided to talk to Gloria about it.

The next morning, when they were working on the horses, Michelle told Gloria about her problems with Ricky, and her desire to leave Tony Marino and the Purple Orchid.

"Ahhh, welllll," Gloria replied, as she took and exhaled a deep breath. "There was a time when Tony and I were very close—I was not only his top dancer, but a verrry clooose friend, if you get my drift. Then I left him under circumstances similar to yours. He wanted to marry me, the dope! I didn't want to marry no Sicilian mobster—I didn't want to marry nobody. I found somebody else, and just walked out."

She continued:

"At first Tony went bonkers. I thought I was due for the Sicilian vespers, whatever that is. But he got over it. A lot of men have declared their eternal love, and then dropped me. Seems to be easy to get over me. I had only one true love, and somehow Tony persuaded him to drop me too."

She shrugged her shoulders and laughed her loud, coarse laugh: "End of my great love affair. End of my career. End of story."

"I'll call Tony and tell him he owes me a favor. He'll let you and your chocolate friend go."

When Michelle talked to Tony that evening, he agreed, but Michelle's interview with him was not pleasant.

"Gloria Van Tassell?" he asked. "Sure. I remember her. Quite a broad. Too old and broad for me, but I was interested. Yeah—I was interested—for a while. Turned out she left me for some playboy wot raised horses out west a here. He became a business associate of mine, and then he dumped her—didn't need 'er. I don't need no broad, neither! And I don't need you and your nigger lesbian friend! Youse can just pick up your checks and get outta here."

Michelle left, stunned by what she had heard. Thelma, who had worked for Gloria, came to Plainfield when Mom died. That was when Gloria quit working for Tony. Who was Gloria's lover who raised horses west of Chicago? And later became a business associate of Tony Marino? Michelle didn't dare ask Gloria or Thelma, because she feared the answer.

She put that question out of her mind, and went with Zane to be interviewed at Elite Escorts in Chicago on North Michigan Avenue. Elite knew Zane, and had a long list of Middle Eastern and African dignitaries who were coming to the city. They also had on their list an African-American homosexual rapper who needed cover while he performed at one of the Chicago night-clubs. Zane sighed, but signed on.

"How about equal opportunity?" she complained. "How about racial integration? How about diversity?"

No luck.

Then the manager turned to Michelle, who flashed her dazzling smile.

"Now this one we can really use," he said. "The auto show will be on at McCormick place. The ad agencies will pay full price to have you stand there and point at their cars. One of their executives will probably want you to go out with him that evening, and you will earn double. Sign here, please."

Michelle learned that each engagement paid $2,500, and she might have two or three engagements a day. The manager explained the no-touch policy. He added that if the girl had a complaint she could go home immediately with her money, and the client had no recourse. Of course, he said, an unhappy client could be bad news, but he thought Michelle would have no difficulty getting new ones.

He added that the Vice Squad kept a close eye on their operations, sometimes sending a ringer as part of a sting. Any misstep with one of their agents would mean discharge of the girl and considerable trouble and expense for the agency.

Thus warned, Michelle decided to sign on, and give Elite Escorts a try. The money would pile up faster, and she could spend more time at Plainfield. The manager sent Michelle and Zane to a safe and comfortable apartment that the agency made available to its girls at a reasonable rent. They agreed to room together and share expenses.

Michelle commuted to Plainfield three days a week, since Biff was willing to pick her up and bring her back. Gloria was doing fine with the horses, although Fatima was proving difficult. Something about Gloria, perhaps a dim memory, bothered her. It was less than a month to Oct. 4, and Michelle was now in the final stretch. There were many things to do at the farm before winter arrived, but they would have to wait.

Actually, Michelle found that working for Elite Escorts was quite interesting, although repelling boarders was an irksome part of it. The high-level businessmen, almost all of them married, and many of them with grandchildren, were men of brains and achievement. They were clumsy, even ludicrous, when they attempted to be Lotharios. When they got past that stage, Michelle enjoyed hearing them talk about business, mergers, stock options, overseas opportunities, and the like. Most of them were genial and liked a good laugh.

They introduced her to their associates as "a friend." Michelle's charm and good looks worked their magic, and others in the group readily accepted her.

At first Michelle did nothing but smile and make conventional remarks. She had not seen much of the world beyond Clarksville, but as she became more comfortable in high circles, she felt able to contribute to the conversation. As a pretty girl, her comments were always well received.

She began educating herself by reading the *Chicago Tribune* regularly. Zane found that Michelle had become surprisingly ready to read books. Sometimes Michelle went with her clients to parties where the wives and girlfriends of other men were present. Zane taught her to play bridge, and she enjoyed woman-talk while playing bridge with the wives. With Zane's help she became a smooth dancer, using all the latest steps. In short, the Homecoming Queen of Clarksville High was becoming a polished young woman, capable of fitting comfortably into the world of status and money.

The most pleasant surprise was Rex Montagu, Dad's friend, who had assisted at the funeral. Working at Elite Escorts meant that Michelle needed clothes of high style and quality. At first she and Clara checked out the mall in Rockford, but Clara admitted that she knew even less about clothes than Michelle. Gloria sent her to an elegant, high-priced women's store in Chicago that she had used at one time. The patrons of the store were mainly well-to-do, middle-aged women. The elderly ladies, who had worked at the store for years, fitted Michelle out with the kind of dress and accessories that one would expect.

When Michelle showed her new (and expensive) outfit to Zane, her friend went into hysterics: "Young lady," she exclaimed, "You goin' to a funeral?" Zane agreed that the dress would serve quite nicely for the Sunday morning service at First Lutheran Church of Clarksville.

When Zane took her shopping, Michelle protested: "Zane, I'm a white girl. White girls don't dress like that—at least, my kind of white girl doesn't."

Then she remembered Rex, and phoned him. Rex stepped in, just as at the funeral, and took over. He was friendly with any number of exclusive dress-makers, and he knew exactly the kind of clothes that would enhance Michelle's already handsome appearance. He also took her to a hairdresser, who cut off her ponytail and gave her a sophisticated hairstyle with short blonde curls. Thus primed and polished, Michelle lived up to Gloria's ideal—the beautiful woman in the TV commercial waiting for the Lincoln Town Car.

In the process, Rex began to see Michelle, not as a cute teenage country girl who rode horses, but as a beautiful young woman potentially fit for high society. He registered with Elite Escorts and took her out four times, introducing her to the delights of the Chicago Symphony, the Lyric Opera, the Art Institute, and Steppenwolf Theatre. They always ate at Chicago's best restaurants.

Michelle, of course, was expensive. When she asked Rex why he utilized the services of Elite Escorts, he replied: "I learned a long time ago that it is cheaper to buy milk than to keep a cow."

Rex was handsome, charming, attentive, and fun. He always seemed to know where to go and what to do. Michelle could enter confidently into the realms of high culture, because Rex would take responsibility, leaving her to enjoy herself. In restaurants, the headwaiter would offer a friendly greeting and have a good table ready. The wine steward received Rex's choices with approval.

Frequently friends of Rex would stop at their table to converse. Rex always introduced Michelle as the daughter of a good friend, who had died recently.

"I have known Michelle," he would say, "since she was a kid. She's grown up very nicely, I think."

The visitor invariably agreed, of course, and Rex would add:

"Michelle's father raised Arabian horses, and she is a splendid horsewoman. When her father was alive, I enjoyed driving out to the farm to ride and to hunt."

"Now that she has become a beautiful young lady, I have another reason to visit Plainfield."

The visitor was left to interpret that last remark for himself.

One evening, walking along Division Street, they were jumped by a mugger, who snatched Michelle's purse and demanded Rex's wallet.

With a quick judo move, Rex flipped the mugger over and threw him to the sidewalk, where he landed on his back. When the man attempted to rise, Rex gave him a quick kick in the kidney. The mugger fled, leaving his loot behind.

Michelle was aghast. Her heart was pounding furiously, while Rex seemed cool as a cucumber.

"Rex, darling," she exclaimed, "he might have had a gun! We could have been shot!"

"I have learned from experience," Rex replied, coolly, "if a mugger doesn't draw his gun when he stops you, he won't use it at all."

With that they continued their stroll. Rex looked as if nothing had happened, but Michelle was so upset that she asked him to take her home immediately.

"I'll tell the agency to refund your money," she said. "They owe you that, and more."

Michelle was now ready to have a man in her life, and her heart began to warm to a man whose poise and culture were so far beyond hers. Although Rex carefully observed the no-touch rule, Michelle did not, holding his arm or hand as they walked along the street, ruffling his hair, punching his shoulder, stroking his back, straightening his tie, giving him little pecks on the cheek, and sitting close to him in the car, her long legs tilted gracefully toward the door. She began calling him "sweetheart" and other affectionate names.

She confided to Zane that she thought she was in love.

"Baby," Zane replied, "you don't know what love is. And, for a while, you don't want to know."

# CHAPTER 9

# *Sybil*

Friday morning, Oct. 1, 1999, was a big day for Michelle. She had enough money in the Clarksville National Bank and Trust to pay off her half of Bubba's mortgage. Earlier that week Lawyer Smart had called to inform her that he had found investors who would put up $120,000 in the form of a mortgage to pay off the other half. As she showered and dressed, Michelle felt a great sense of relief, personal satisfaction, and freedom.

She was relieved that her career as a stripper and paid escort was finished. It had been an interesting experience, and she had learned a lot about the world beyond Clarksville. She had maintained her own personal standards and integrity. But she did not like the commercial sex business, which she found degrading, to men as well as women. Her personal satisfaction came from taking control of her life: she had made a big decision, and had seen it through to a successful conclusion. She was now free from the clutches of Bubba Grubbs and could return to the life and horses that she loved at Plainfield.

After breakfast, Gloria and Biff left to return to Park Ridge. Michelle knew how much she owed to them, and expressed her gratitude as completely as she could.

"Remember what I told you about DNA," Gloria said. "It is the secret to understanding men, and women too, I suppose, although I never thought much about that."

As Biff started the car, she called out to Michelle:

"And keep that little black dress. You may need it some day."

"Mickey," Thelma said, as the big 1979 Buick disappeared down the road, "you probably won't need me here much longer. You're grown up now, and the lady of the house. Plainfield ain't had a lady of the house for six years."

Tears welled up in her eyes.

"I never knowed the first lady of the house, your Mom," she said, "but everyone who knowed her loved her. Now Plainfield has a new lady of the house—someone worthy to be her successor. I hate to leave, but one of the secrets of living is to know when to let go."

"Thelma, Thelma," Michelle replied, her eyes moist, as she gave her a big hug.

"Plainfield won't be the same without you. We've been through a lot together, and you have taken Mom's place as well as anyone could."

"I want you to stay as long as you want to stay. I want you to go when you are ready to go."

"For the present, let's leave it at that."

When Michelle drove into town, her first stop was at the bank, where she withdrew $120,000 in the form of a certified check made out to Bubba Grubbs. Then she crossed the street to Lawyer Smart's office.

"Well, Michelle," he said with a big smile on his face, "you made it. God-dammit, you made it!—Please excuse my exclamation mark."

Michelle noted with surprise that he had a crooked smile, just like Waldo's.

She gave him the certified check.

"I would rather not deal with Bubba personally," she said. "I prefer that you deliver my check and the money from the new mortgage to Bubba. It will be a great relief to have nothing more to do with him."

"No problem," Lawyer Smart responded, "I'll take care of Bubba. Now on to your new mortgage."

Automatically he went into his attorney-client mode. He turned to his desk, ruffled some papers, came up with something, discarded it, and found the mortgage.

"Ah, here it is," he exclaimed, knowing all the time where it was.

He looked it over, pursing his lips, although he knew very well what was in it. "Here is a mortgage for $120,000 on Plainfield, the land and buildings."

He paused. He had learned over the years that is necessary to give a jury ample time to let his words sink in. He applied the same principle to clients in his office.

"You will find that the payments are not onerous," he continued. "Bubba charged your Dad a ferocious rate of interest, with a short time for repayment of the principal. The interest rate on your new mortgage is low, and the mortgage runs for thirty years, although you may repay it sooner, without penalty."

"That's terrific," Michelle said. "I don't know how you did it, but I'll take it!"

Lawyer Smart cleared his throat, and looked out the window. He turned back to Michelle.

"The investors who have provided the money for the mortgage," he said, clearing his throat again, "wish to remain anonymous. You will make your monthly payments to me. Make your checks payable to 'Michelle Mortgage Trust/Clarksville National Bank and Trust.' That is all you need to know."

"Now please sign here," he said, covering the part with the signatures of the investors.

As Michelle signed she said: "I know I can make the payments. It is so wonderful to be free of Bubba Grubbs and the pressure for money. Now I can live again!"

She turned to Lawyer Smart and gave him a lipstick kiss on the cheek, supplemented by a squeeze.

"My thanks to you," she said, flashing her winning smile. "And to the investors, whoever they are. Everyone has been so helpful to me since Dad died! I can hardly believe it."

Michelle floated back to Plainfield on a cloud of euphoria, until she turned into the drive that led to the farm place. Then she saw two cars of the sheriff's police, lights flashing, parked in front of the house. Policemen were searching the barn and the paddock, and roping them off with yellow tape.

As she drove up and parked, Thelma rushed toward her.

"Mickey, Mickey," she exclaimed, "Sybil has been shot! With a bow and arrow. She is dead. Nobody knows who did it, but they are trying to find out."

Michelle rushed to the barn. She looked on with horror at Sybil, who lay, stretched out in her stall, in a pool of blood, with an arrow in her neck, just above the shoulder. The other horses were in the paddock, in a state of consternation. Akbar was frantic with fury, and Michelle feared that he might attack the police, as he had attacked Bubba.

"Don't touch anything," a policeman said. "We left the arrow in place, because she was dead when we got here. Do you have any idea who might have done this, and why?"

Michelle was numb. She didn't want to talk to anyone, especially the police. She had some suspicions, but she was too shocked to think clearly. Tony Marino? Ricky? Bubba? Sonny?

She felt weak. "Take me back into the house," she said to Thelma, who helped her up the walk and porch steps.

"I just need to lie down a while."

Michelle stretched out on the bed in her clothes. She felt a chill, although it was a warm day, and pulled the bedspread over her. For a long time she tossed and turned, her mind a whirlwind of thoughts and anxieties. A pervasive fear ran through her body. Somewhere a cruel enemy lurked, determined to hurt her.

Her fear was intensified by an acute sense of isolation. Suddenly she realized how much she missed the camaraderie of the previous four months: Thelma's "How did it go last night?" when she came down for breakfast; Gloria's hearty earthiness and obvious delight in farm life; and Biff's silent presence, as he drove her to and from work. She missed the street-wise remarks of Zane and the bright lights of the Purple Orchid; she had felt a sense of power, as she performed in the spotlight, all eyes focused on her. She missed the variety and sociability of the big money world of Elite Escorts.

Especially Michelle missed Rex—strong, gentle, and sophisticated—and the high culture that he had opened up to her.

Michelle slept for about an hour, and woke up feeling refreshed. She was back in charge again and ready to deal with the immediate problem of Sybil. When she walked down to the barn, the sheriff was there with a detective and a photographer, who had just completed their work. The arrow had been removed from Sybil's body. The detective showed Michelle the long, heavy bow-hunting arrow with its jagged steel tip.

"It took a powerful bow to shoot this arrow," he said, "and a strong arm to pull the bow. We had to push the arrow all the way through to get it out. We'll try to find out where this arrow was purchased and who bought it. We need to take the body in for an autopsy."

Michelle nodded her assent.

The detective took Michelle to a clump of trees at the back of the barn, and showed her footmarks in the ground.

"We figure the perpetrator hid in these trees during the night," he said, "and waited until you left the house. Then he slipped around to the stable door, which had the top half open, and shot directly into the horse's stall. There's no sign that he tried to retrieve his arrow—probably to avoid fingerprints. One man couldn't 'a pulled it out, anyway."

He pointed toward the river.

"He musta scooted back into the trees and made a dash across the pasture to the river. We can follow his footprints in places, but they end at the river. Since the river is low this time of year, he probably waded a considerable distance before he climbed out of it. The ground on the other side is hard and dry, and we could find no footprints."

"Sorry, Miss," he concluded, "she sure was a beautiful horse. My uncle had an Arabian, once. I learned to ride on her. Real friendly horse."

Thelma, who had followed Michelle to the barn, chimed in.

"I heard a lot of noise from the horses, just a little after Michelle left. They was running wildly around the paddock, and the stallion was in a mighty rage. For the last coupla days, people have reported seeing a cougar down along the river. I thought maybe the cougar had showed up. After a while the horses settled down."

Michelle explained that Sybil was in her stall because she was again in heat. Akbar's earlier effort had not taken hold, as often happens the first time a filly is bred.

By this time Charley Foxx had turned up, his ever-present hat tilted rakishly to one side.

"Michelle," he said, "the sheriff will do all he can to find out who did this. And I'll prosecute to the limits of the law. I'm working on some things right now that could pay off. You might find all of this upsetting, so I'll deal with you through Lawyer Smart, if that's O.K. with you. You will have to give a deposition, and sign some other papers."

He looked her straight in the eye:

"Someone has it in for you," he said, "and may strike again. He could try to burn your barn with an incendiary arrow, or inflict some other damage. I don't think you, personally, are in danger. The sheriff will post an officer out here for the next few nights, just in case. You won't be completely safe until we catch this guy."

He paused, choosing his words carefully.

"Don't forget our previous conversation," he said. "I still need your help on that matter."

Michelle began to think that maybe she should have been more forthcoming when Foxx had asked her to talk about the party at the lake.

At that moment, she saw a sleek sports car coming up the driveway. It was Rex.

She ran to him, exclaiming breathlessly "Rex! You came just in time! I need you, Rex. I'm so frightened."

The confidence that Michelle had developed over the previous four months had evaporated completely. She needed someone strong to lean on. And some quirk of fate had led Rex to Plainfield that day.

"What's going on here," Rex asked. "I leave the crime-ridden streets of the city and drive out into the peaceful countryside, and I find this!"

Foxx and sheriff's police were just leaving, although one man remained to protect the site.

Michelle explained what had happened as she and Rex walked up to the house. He stopped and looked around the farm place.

"I haven't been here for a long time," he remarked. "The place looks great!"

They sat down on the veranda, and Thelma brought coffee and Danish rolls, baked that morning by Lena.

"Rex, sweetheart," Michelle said, "don't leave me now. Stay for a few days, anyway. I don't know what to think or do about this, but I need someone to advise me and keep me company. And I'm scared. There's somebody out there who hates me. Please say you'll stay."

"I've got to make a couple of phone calls," Rex replied, "but I can stay for a day or two."

Thelma's face showed that she was not pleased when Michelle informed her that Rex would be staying with them, but she readied the guest room, and after that stayed out of sight.

"Let's go for a ride, darling," Rex said, "it's such a glorious day. Might take your mind off your troubles."

Michelle fetched a set of Dad's riding clothes, which fitted Rex perfectly, and donned her own gear. They saddled their horses, and rode out into the pasture, which led to the river.

Michelle felt a great sense of liberation—from loneliness and fear—as she rode with Rex at her side. Rex was an excellent rider, but he had difficulty keeping pace with her as they galloped across the countryside. From her childhood days, Michelle had always been confident—even reckless—on the back of a horse. Freed momentarily from her anxieties, she gave way to her natural ebullience and rode with a daring that worried Rex.

"Let's stop here, darling," Rex called, as they approached the river. "The horses need a breather, and, frankly, so do I."

It was a beautiful autumn day—the best time of the year in northern Illinois, some say. They stopped and stretched out on the grass, under an ancient sycamore tree on a high spot that overlooked the rolling plains and the river below. The cornfields, ripe for the harvest, were sheets of pale gold, mingled with russet patches of dead-ripe soybeans. The landscape was varied by the bright green of the pastures and the deep green of alfalfa, now ready for its third cutting. The exuberance of nature was confined within orderly bounds by clumps of trees and shrubs that followed the fence lines. Below them, the river, a ribbon of greenery and fall colors, wound its eccentric way into the distance.

"This is wonderful," Rex replied. "And so different from the clamor and turmoil of the city. I wish that a day like today could last forever!"

In the previous four months, Michelle had learned to take charge of her life. Impulsively, she spoke words that had been in her heart for some time.

"Why not, Rex," she asked. "Let's get married. We could be together always, right here at Plainfield."

She seized his arm, and looked him straight in the eye.

"I love you, Rex," she said. "Your presence makes me happy. The sun won't always shine, but we would be together on the dark days, too."

Rex was taken aback.

"What about the no-touch rule?" he asked with a smile. "Would that still apply?"

Michelle threw her arms around him, and kissed him full on the lips. There was not much response from Rex, but that could be attributed to surprise.

"Hold it, hold it," Rex exclaimed, pushing her away. "I need time to clear my head."

He looked into the distance, as he collected his thoughts. Then he turned to Michelle and put his arm around her.

"Michelle," he said, "you have made me happier than any woman I have ever known. I have waited too long to find you, but now that you are here and close to me, I know my time has come."

With that he returned her kiss, although without much passion. Michelle didn't know about such things. Rex was the first man that she had ever kissed, apart from her father. Her relationship with Sonny had been one of attacker and defender, and she had always managed to hold him off.

With a happy heart, Michelle returned to Plainfield, Rex at her side, where she announced triumphantly to Thelma that she and Rex were to be married.

"Tell Lena it's time for dinner," she said, "I'm hungry."

# CHAPTER 10

# *Rex*

Rex did not seemed pleased with Lena's dinner of meat loaf, mashed potatoes, peas, and apple pie, but Michelle ate heartily. Rex said that he was not accustomed to eating that much at noon. When dinner was finished it was time to look after the horses, who had been neglected in the excitement of Sybil's murder, Rex's arrival, and the impromptu ride in the country. Akbar had calmed down, but Fatima was devastated. She had not seen the crime, but she had heard the men loading Sybil's body on a truck, and had seen the body carried away. Michelle embraced her neck, as Fatima rested her head on Michelle's shoulder. She and Michelle exchanged little cooing sounds, which came from Fatima and Michelle imitated to perfection. Michelle knew and understood horses, and Fatima knew that her loving mistress shared her pain.

After that it was necessary to do all the chores that came with keeping horses. Luke had already fed and watered them, and Michelle gave them their daily brushing. Ben saddled and walked them, and Rex rode them around the track. When these chores were finished, it was time to shower and dress for supper. Lena served cold meat loaf sandwiches and potato salad, favorites of Michelle. Rex said that he was still full from dinner.

Since it was a cool evening, Michelle asked Rex if he would light a fire in the fireplace. As the flames leaped upward, they sat side by side on the sofa. Michelle cuddled close to Rex, feeling the strength of his wiry male body. Rex seemed slightly uncomfortable with togetherness. When Michelle said that she would speak to Rev. Wiseman about the wedding, Rex interrupted.

"Look, Michelle," he said, "I don't want a church wedding, and I don't want to be married in Clarksville. I don't know anybody here, and they don't know me. My friends are in Chicago; some of them were friends of your father, too, and came here for the funeral. They won't want to drive out here again. I would like to be married in the Cook County courthouse, with a nice lunch afterward. When we get back from our honeymoon, we'll put on a big party here, at Plainfield, for the local people."

Michelle was startled by Rex's remarks. Her idea of a wedding was a simple affair, like Clara and Rusty. But Rex insisted, and she had become accustomed to having him take the lead in their relationship.

Rex had another reason.

"When I called one of my friends in Chicago," he said, "he told me that he knew of a high-class riding trip in the Canadian Rockies. The tour leaves next week. He thinks there may be room for two more."

Rex grew animated: "Darling," he said, "darling Michelle, that would be a wonderful honeymoon for us. We both like to ride, and the Rockies will be splendid this time of year—probably some snowfall in the higher elevations. Please say that you will go. We can leave from O'Hare immediately after the wedding."

Michelle didn't know what to think. Getting married had turned out to be more complicated for her than for Clara and Rusty. She began to warm to the idea. She had never seen mountains before. She had never been on a jet plane either, and she looked forward eagerly to the experience.

"As usual," she said to Rex, "you are way ahead of me. Why not? I think I can make arrangements for the horses."

"O. K.," she declared in a burst of enthusiasm, "let's go!"

As Michelle had expected, Gloria was willing to come back to the farm for a week, and Biff had nothing better to do, anyway. Ben would saddle, brush, and walk the horses, and a local high school boy was willing to give them a daily workout after school. Luke would feed and water them, and Gloria would make herself useful. Rex made all arrangements for the wedding and the trip.

The next morning they drove into Chicago to take care of the legal formalities. The wedding was set for 10:00 a.m. on the earliest possible day. Rex planned a champagne lunch at a nearby restaurant. At 3:00 p.m. they would leave from O'Hare Field for Calgary.

When he drove Michelle back to Plainfield, Rex said that he had to return to the city on business: there was a large garment convention in town, which he had to attend. He said he would be back to pick her up early the day of the wedding. Then he left. Michelle was understandably disappointed, but she had many things to do. She called Clara and they went to a nearby mall, where Michelle bought new clothes for the wedding and a new riding outfit. She also bought a wool plaid shirt, heavy denims, and warm flannel pajamas. She looked at a coy bridal nighty, but decided it was not right for the Rockies in October.

Michelle knew that she should talk to Rev. Wiseman about her wedding plans, but she felt very uncomfortable as she entered his office. She told him about Rex, exaggerating considerably the circumstances and extent of their acquaintance. She apologized for being married in Chicago, rather than First Lutheran, but hastened to add that after the honeymoon they would have a reception, where the pastor and the members of congregation could celebrate their wedding. Most members had already seen Rex at the funeral, although he had been fully occupied with the visitors.

"I hope you will understand," Michelle said, defensively. "I love Rex and he loves me. We are quite different in age and interests, but so were my father and mother. I know we can be happy together."

Rev. Wiseman was understandably disturbed by this sudden news. He knew some things about Michelle's father and mother, but they were sealed by the confidentiality of the confessional. More important, he knew nothing about Rex, but he was fully aware of the simplicity and naiveté of Michelle.

"Michelle, my dear," he said. "There is a saying: 'Marry in haste and repent at leisure.'"

He paused for a moment.

"When you came to me and told me you wanted to be a strip-tease dancer, I was not pleased. But I knew your upbringing and values, and I gave my reluctant consent. Well, you seem to have accomplished your purpose: you made a courageous decision and you saved Plainfield. Based on that, I must again give my blessing. Come here, my sweet girl," he said.

Rev. Wiseman invited Michelle to kneel with him, and together they repeated the Lord's Prayer. The pastor rose, and helped Michelle to her feet.

"When you are married," he said, "I hope you will come to see me, with your husband. I think we should have a little talk about marriage in general, and Christian marriage in particular."

Michelle was glad she had come, although the pastor's words were unsettling. When she got home she busied herself with the horses, and her uneasiness went away.

Early on their wedding morning, Rex turned up at Plainfield, looking tense.

"Come'on, Michelle," he said, "we mustn't be late." He put her luggage in the trunk and opened the door on the passenger side.

"Sorry I didn't get here last night, darling," he said, as she got in the car, "but when you have five stores scattered over 150 miles, it takes time to visit them all. Anyway, we're off!"

He started the car and dashed down the drive before Michelle had time to say goodbye to Thelma, Gloria, and Biff.

As they cruised along the interstate and took the expressway into the city, Michelle sat close to Rex, admiring the skill with which he maneuvered through traffic.

"We'll have a great time, Michelle," he said, "you'll love riding in the mountains. Exhilarating but tiring, for both horse and rider. Fortunately, we'll have first-class food and accommodations."

The wedding itself took about fifteen minutes. There were fewer guests than Michelle had expected, and she felt out of place being married before strangers. Her sense of uneasiness strengthened when she saw Ricky Marino smirking at the back of the room. She was relieved when he left early and did not stay for the receiving line or lunch. The lunch was excellent but the congratulations and conversation were rather forced. As soon as they were finished, Rex asked that they be excused and they hurried off to O'Hare Field.

Michelle found the flight exciting, especially the view of the broad plains of North Dakota and Alberta. Her eyes sparkled with anticipation as they landed in Calgary, where they met the other members of the tour while they waited for their luggage. Then a bus took them to their base, a fine hotel nestled by a mountain lake.

"The view is breathtaking, Rex," Michelle commented, as they went for a walk after dinner. "The people in our group seem very nice." She took his arm and kissed him on the cheek.

"Thanks for bringing me here," she said.

In the hotel, some members of the tour were playing bridge. When they discovered that Rex was a master bridge player, they invited him to join them.

"I hope you don't mind, dear," Rex said. "Bridge in the evening is part of every first-class tour."

Michelle sat down beside a pleasant man of about thirty. His name was Roger Torgerson, and he operated a riding school at Moose River, Minnesota. Roger's wife, Susan, was a product of the horsy country of Virginia, and was a superb bridge player, as well as rider. She was Rex's partner. Roger was a plain, sturdy, Minnesota-Norwegian-Lutheran, who loved horses but did not play cards. Soon Michelle and Roger were talking horseman's talk, and the time passed quickly.

By 9:00 p.m. Roger was tired and went off to bed, leaving Michelle sitting alone. She was drooping too: she had been married, met strangers at lunch, taken her first flight by jet, and spent several hours by bus getting to the hotel. She had enjoyed seeing mountains, but was unaccustomed to the altitude. Rex noticed that she was alone.

"Look here, Michelle," he said, "we want to finish this rubber. Why don't you go off to bed, and I'll join you as soon as I can. Here's the key to the room."

"Thanks, Rex," Michelle replied, "I'm sorry for fading out so early, but it has been a busy day."

As she got ready for bed and put on her flannel pajamas, Michelle did not know what to expect on her wedding night. She assumed that she and Rex would have sexual intercourse, but she had no idea how the process would begin or proceed. The girls at Clarksville High had talked about this, sharing tales from other girls, especially about painful penetration and blood on the sheets. Michelle, of course, was a virgin, and she felt anxious about satisfying a man of the world like Rex. She stretched out on the bed, waiting for Rex, and immediately fell asleep.

When Michelle awoke the next morning, she discovered that Rex had put her under the blankets, but there was no sign that he had actually slept in the bed. A pillow and blanket were on the couch; presumably he had slept there. In a few minutes Rex came into the room.

"Michelle, darling," he said, giving her a peck on the forehead, "you must get dressed right away. We're ready to go. Your horse is saddled. The other people are waiting."

Hurriedly Michelle splashed water on her face and pulled on her riding clothes and boots. There was no time for breakfast. The other members of the group were already in the saddle. They exchanged wise looks as Michelle emerged, apologizing. Obviously the young bride had been kept busy on her wedding night.

As the group climbed into the mountains, Rex was the life of the party. He rode back and forth, talking to the other riders, helping and encouraging several senior couples who had taken on more than they could handle. With advanced riders, Rex played "chicken," dashing up steep slopes and daring others to follow.

Michelle was a good rider, but she had ridden only on the rolling plains of northern Illinois, and was unaccustomed to riding in the mountains. Her horse was balky and the saddle was different.

"You'd better stay on the trails, Michelle," Rex said, "until you become more comfortable on these slopes."

Fortunately Roger, more a teacher of horsemanship than a rider, took Michelle in hand and taught her the techniques of mountain riding. Susan was able to match Rex, and by lunchtime they were high overhead on a rocky crag. They waved sandwiches, which they had remembered to take with them, at the group of riders having lunch below.

The first day the tour group rode to a rough-hewn lodge, built especially for tour rides. The lodge would be the center for their rides into the mountains. They arrived about 5:00 p.m. By that time the sun had dropped behind the mountain, darkness had fallen, and a chill wind had sprung up. The cooks had prepared a hearty trail dinner, and afterward the cowboy guides entertained with western songs and jokes.

When bridge was proposed, Rex declined.

"Sorry," he said, "I'm pooped. I hate to think how my horse must be feeling."

He turned to Michelle.

"Darling," he said, "I don't want to take you away from the fun. The trail dinner with songs is part of every tour."

With that he left. Michelle was non-plussed, since Rex had made it clear that he did not want her to come along. She followed after, and joined him in the room.

"Rex," she said, "this is our honeymoon. I want to love you. I'm tired too. Let's get in bed together."

Rex was irritated by her insistence.

"Listen, Michelle," he said in a tense voice, "when I say I'm tired, that means I want to sleep. Suit yourself, but I do not want to hear any more about this."

Quickly he put on his pajamas and got into bed, his face to the wall. Michelle could not face the embarrassment of returning to the group by herself, obviously rejected by her husband. She sat on the couch for a while, and then got ready for bed.

As she looked at Rex, who was sleeping, Michelle realized that he was "old." Asleep, he was nothing like the dashing gentleman whose company she had enjoyed at the Lyric Opera or walking down Michigan Avenue on a warm summer evening. Or the bold rider on the steep slopes of the Canadian Rockies.

His face was sunken and his skin a pallid yellow. He breathed noisily through his mouth. A sinking feeling crept over Michelle. She crawled into bed, not touching him, and lay awake for a long time, wondering why she was there.

The next morning Rex was his usual dapper self. Embarrassed by the night before, he made special efforts to be nice to Michelle, with plenty of "darlings" and "Michelle dears." On the slopes, Michelle was now able to keep up with Rex and Susan, although she had to be cautioned occasionally to avoid tricky rocks and other hazards. She was accustomed to her saddle, and, with a more experienced rider, her horse began performing beautifully. The scenery was magnificent.

As Michelle's youthful vitality emerged, and Rex and Susan began to look tired, she became the top rider of the group and had a marvelous time. As usual, she was friendly to everyone, and was popular with the less experienced riders, especially several elderly couples who were having difficulty coping.

With her confidence back, Michelle decided that she would talk to Rex that night about his seeming lack of sexual interest. With the group, at meals or on the trail, he was the embodiment of the attentive, loving husband. At night he allowed Michelle to go to bed first, and slept on the sofa. She hoped that he was merely shy, and would come around with patience and encouragement. Plainfield had once owned a stallion who was slow to perform.

Rex was embarrassed and apologetic.

"Michelle, dear," he said, "please realize that I need time. I love you, and I want to be intimate with you, but I have lived a long time as a bachelor. I am not accustomed to having a woman with me, day and night. Mountain air and strenuous riding are exhilarating, but they leave me exhausted. I realize now that we should not have taken such a strenuous honeymoon."

He took her in his arms.

"Please believe me, dearest Michelle," he pleaded, "when we get home and back to our normal lives, things will be different."

Although Michelle enjoyed the tour very much, they had an unspoken agreement that she would sleep in the bed, and he would sleep on the couch. She was still a virgin when they returned to the base hotel, where buses were waiting to take the group to the Calgary airport. As the group climbed into the airport bus, Rex took Michelle aside.

"Look, Michelle," he said with considerable embarrassment, "I hate to ask this of you, but before we left two of my friends from Chicago mentioned that they would like to have me go with them hunting bighorn mountain sheep. They are here and waiting to leave. This is something that I have always wanted to do. Now that I'm married, I'll probably never have another chance. I have arranged for you to stay at the hotel until we get back. I'll be gone three or four days."

He put both arms on her shoulders, looking at her with a coaxing smile. He saw the look of amazement on her face.

"I know this comes as a surprise, but I didn't know for sure that they would show up until now. For me, this expedition will make our first trip together complete. And wouldn't the curly-horned head of a mountain ram look good over our fireplace? I won't go if you don't want me to go, but you have to make up your mind right away. Please wait for me here. I don't want you flying into O'Hare tonight by yourself."

Michelle was astounded at this sudden news. She looked and saw the two other hunters, dressed in hunting clothes, waiting with their big-game rifles and Land Rover. Her heart sank. She was too tired of Rex's treatment of her to protest.

"O.K.," she said wearily, "I'll wait here."

Every bit the gentleman, Rex took her luggage and escorted her into the hotel as if she were the Queen of Sheba.

"This is my wife," he announced proudly, "I spoke to you about her earlier. She will stay here until I get back. I trust you will show her every courtesy."

With that, Rex left with his hunting companions. A porter took Michelle to her room, which was cold. Apologetically, the kindly porter said that he would ask about the heating.

When she had unpacked her luggage, Michelle rang the desk to ask about dinner. No one answered. As she walked down the dimly lit stairs to inquire, she realized that the hotel was empty. Most of the lights were turned off. She found the porter, who told her that no tours were scheduled for a week, and the hotel had only a skeleton staff.

Since she was hungry, the porter directed her to the kitchen, where she found a worker cleaning up. The woman said that she could provide soup and sandwiches on a room service basis, but that no meals would be cooked until the next tour arrived. Quickly the woman prepared a modest lunch, which Michelle ate in the kitchen. The woman realized Michelle's predicament and expressed her sympathy. She said that she was going off work and would not be back until 10:00 a.m. the next morning.

Michelle felt better after she had eaten, and decided to take a walk. When she headed to the door, the porter called out to her.

"Better not go out by yourself, Miss," he said. "They's bears out there. When they's hungry, they come down from the mountain to raid the garbage cans. They ain't no garbage today, so they'll be in a really ugly mood."

When Michelle returned to her room, total despair swept over her. She had been abandoned in a dark, cold, empty building. She was frightened—through and through. Worse, she felt utterly rejected. She must have been unworthy in some way, she thought. She blamed herself.

"What could I have done differently?" she asked.

She fell on her bed. She was too devastated to weep. The next three days were a blur, ending in collapse. When she regained consciousness, she was in a hospital room in Calgary. She heard a doctor in a white coat speaking to Rex.

"I'm afraid," the doctor said, "your wife has had some kind of a breakdown, aggravated by a cold room and lack of food. She must have been lying unconscious in that hotel room for some time."

"Not entirely," Rex replied. "When I returned from my hunting expedition the desk clerk told me that she had been wandering aimlessly through the hotel for several days. A woman in the kitchen provided her with sandwiches and salad, but she told me that Michelle ate very little. Poor thing. I feel terrible that this has happened."

"Did you have any reason to think that something like this might take place?" the doctor asked.

"I always knew that Michelle was a high-strung, temperamental girl," Rex replied. "I probably should have taken that into consideration, because she is young—only eighteen. But she wanted so much to go on this trip. I thought it would be a good way to begin our marriage."

The doctor gave Rex a stern look.

"Frankly," he said, "I'm surprised that you would leave a young girl alone in an empty hotel while you went off hunting. How did that happen?"

"That was Michelle's idea too," Rex replied. "When our honeymoon did not go well, she said she needed time by herself to think. She encouraged me to go: she wanted a ram's head to put over the fireplace. As to the hotel, Michelle loved it when we arrived. I did not know that it was deserted."

"Sometimes these things happen on a honeymoon," the doctor said. "One purpose of a honeymoon is to provide an opportunity for the bride and groom to get to know each other on an intimate, twenty-four hour basis."

He paused for a moment before introducing a sensitive subject.

"Tell me," the doctor asked, "did you and your bride have sexual relations during your honeymoon?"

Rex looked embarrassed.

"No," he stated firmly. "Michelle wanted nothing to do with me. She seemed frightened to have sex."

"Sometimes these young girls get negative ideas about intercourse," the doctor replied. "They have heard tales of painful penetration, blood on the sheets, and worse. The problem is often aggravated by a young husband, who is impatient and regards hesitance on the part of his bride as a challenge to his manhood."

"Fortunately," the doctor continued, "you seem to have taken a mature approach to the problem. Just be patient. Sometimes it takes several months for a bride to accept her husband."

"Trust me," he chuckled, "once she has given way, you'll have trouble fending her off!"

The doctor became very businesslike.

"She should stay here for another twenty-four hours. She is young and healthy, and will recover quickly. She should be ready to return home tomorrow."

With that he left. Rex remained in the room, and sat down in a chair for a few minutes, before leaving too.

Michelle had heard the entire conversation, and now knew what she had to do. Rev. Wiseman had been right: "Marry in haste; repent at leisure." She was silent on the return trip, pretending to be ill. Rex made no effort to speak to her.

When they got back to Plainfield, Thelma, Gloria, and Biff were waiting anxiously. Rex had not informed them that their return would be delayed. When she saw Michelle in her weakened condition, Thelma put her in bed immediately.

Rex offered no explanations. After Thelma had left the bedroom, he said to Michelle:

"Michelle, darling. Please listen to me. I have to go into the city for a few days, to take care of business that has been neglected during our trip. When I get back, we'll both work seriously to get our problems straightened out."

Then he left.

When Michelle heard his car disappear down the road, she leaped out of bed, pulled on her denims, and went to the barn to check on the horses. They were doing fine. They were glad to see her back, although they had become accustomed to Gloria's ministrations.

Then Michelle returned to the house, changed, and drove into Clarksville. First she stopped to see Lawyer Smart, and then she prepared to face Rev. Wiseman.

She had taken charge of her life before, and she was determined to do so again.

# CHAPTER 11

# *Sonny*

When Michelle stepped into Lawyer Smart's office, he was startled at her gaunt, pale appearance. "Michelle," he said, "what has happened? Have you been sick? Have you had an accident?"

"Worse than that," Michelle replied. "I have had a personal disaster, and I need you to help me get out of it."

Painfully and haltingly, she told the story of her marriage to Rex and the trip to the Canadian Rockies.

"Michelle," Smart replied, stunned, "you have been deceived and cruelly mistreated."

"Would you like to have this fraudulent marriage annulled?" he asked.

Michelle nodded agreement.

Smoothly Smart clicked into his lawyer-client mode.

"Society has rightly decided," he pontificated, "that marriage should not be entered into lightly, or dissolved without good reason. Marriage involves many complicated legal matters, and so does an annulment. I'll take care of that, and get it done as expeditiously as possible. I won't go into the details of the law and the procedures; you have enough to think about as it is."

He paced around the room, collecting his thoughts, although he knew perfectly well what he intended to say.

"I know nothing about this man, Rex Montagu," he said, pronouncing the name with obvious contempt. "I saw him at your father's funeral with people who inspired mistrust. He may be some kind of a gold digger. On the other hand, he may be a decent fellow who will be willing to make the best of a bad situation and get out. I shall find out soon enough."

"There is one thing that you must do. I will get a court order to prevent Montagu from contacting you in any way. You must have nothing whatsoever to do with him."

He chuckled as he recalled Akbar's tangle with Bubba Grubbs' car:

"If your husband—who is no husband—turns up at Plainfield, turn that stallion of yours loose on him."

He laughed heartily at his joke, as Michelle waited patiently for him to get back to business.

"Under these circumstances," Smart continued, "I am reluctant to bring back other unpleasant memories, but I want you to know that Charley Foxx, our state's attorney, is in touch with me concerning Sonny's attack on you at the party last June. In Illinois law, the crime that we used to call rape is now referred to as sexual assault. Whatever they call it, you will probably be expected to give testimony in open court."

He drew himself up to his full courtroom dignity.

"When that time comes," he said, "you must have the courage to do your duty."

Michelle nodded agreement, as she turned to leave.

"One more thing," Lawyer Smart said, as he ushered her to the door.

"I will call Dr. Carey right now, and tell him you are coming. You need a physical examination for a variety of reasons, but one is that I must have medical evidence to support your claim that you and your husband did not have sexual intercourse. You should also be examined for general health reasons. If I may say so, you look ill at present."

"I have been ill," Michelle replied, "desperately ill, but I am recovering. O.K. I'll go to Dr. Carey's office next."

Dr. Carey was his usual smiling self, until he got a good look at Michelle.

"Good grief," he said, "what has happened to you?"

"I have been ill," Michelle replied, "but I am recovering."

Then she told the story of her marriage and honeymoon. It came a little easier this time. She added that Lawyer Smart needed a medical examination to support his request for an annulment.

"Well, well, well," Dr. Carey exclaimed, when Michelle had finished. "You've been through the mill, haven't you? We'll see what we can do about that! I'll just take a look."

When his examination was finished, the good doctor assisted Michelle to her feet.

"Judging from appearances," he said, "you are as much a virgin now as the day you were born. However, I shall need some blood tests. The results should be back in a few days."

"Of course, I believe your story," he added, "but we can't be too careful. Sometimes young brides find themselves pregnant, or with a venereal disease, and don't even know that intercourse has taken place. Working with horses, as you do, that is highly unlikely. But we must take all necessary steps to protect your health, and convince a court of law that your marriage should be declared null and void."

With that, he gave Michelle a prescription to help her feel and sleep better, and extended his sympathy and best wishes.

"Your bad experience can have long-term effects on your mental and physical health," he said.

"Even if you feel now that you are recovering, your feelings of anxiety and depression are likely to return. You have always been strong and healthy, mentally and physically. I will do my best to get you through this trauma."

Michelle's next step was the most difficult: a visit to Rev. Wiseman. Her visits with Lawyer Smart and Dr. Carey had given her encouragement. With Rev. Wiseman, she would have to admit that she had ignored his advice and plunged into a dreadful marriage. Sometimes it is easier to admit that one has been a sinner than to admit that one has been a fool.

For the third time the scenario was repeated. Rev. Wiseman was startled by her appearance; she told her story; Rev. Wiseman responded with sympathy and understanding; and he offered his own prescription.

"Michelle," he said, "you have acted impulsively and paid for it, but most people—myself included—have done that on one occasion or another. You probably will recover physically faster than you will recover spiritually."

"Let me assure you," he continued, "that there is nothing wrong with you that time, effort, and prayer will not heal. You are still the same wonderful girl that you always were, although bruised by a devastating experience. The ultimate sin is to despair of yourself and God's willingness to help you."

"It will not be easy," he continued. "You will have to face dark thoughts that can come upon you at any time. There is nothing so terrifying," he added, "as the darkness of the soul."

"The best advice I can give you," he concluded, "is to return to your usual life. Hard work is good for the body and the soul. You have wonderful friends;

open yourself to them and let them help you. Clara will be at your side when you need her."

"Then there are the horses: I know how important they are to you. When you feel disgusted with yourself, or discouraged with your future, remember that the horses depend on you. If you begin by loving and helping your horses, you will move easily to loving and helping your friends, and from there you will end up loving yourself and loving God."

By this time, tears were flowing down Michelle's cheeks. Rev. Wiseman rose to his feet, although Michelle remained seated. He put both hands on her head and repeated the benediction that she had heard every Sunday since childhood:

"The Lord bless thee, and keep thee.

The Lord make his face shine upon thee, and be gracious unto thee.

The Lord lift up his countenance upon thee, and give thee peace."

Michelle felt much better as she drove back to Plainfield. When she got there she gave a cheery greeting to Thelma, a big hug to Gloria, and planted a kiss on Biff's bald pate, as he loaded the luggage to return to Park Ridge.

She pulled on her oft-washed denims, checked with Lena in the kitchen to find out what she was making for dinner, gave a wave and a smile to Luke, who was taking a load of manure to spread on the pasture, looked in on Ben, who wasn't doing much of anything, and got to work with the horses.

With her marriage defunct and in the process of annulment, Michelle's brief burst of confidence soon dwindled. She again experienced the gnawing sense of worthlessness that turned all her former joys to dust. As before, she turned to Clara for emotional support. Although she was six months pregnant, and her slight build was not likely to carry the child full term, Clara did not hesitate. She stayed at Plainfield for days at a time.

The horses shared Michelle's distress. They sensed that something was amiss at Plainfield. They had been upset by the shooting of Sybil and Michelle's sudden disappearance with Rex. Their anxiety was seen in the evident satisfaction with which they welcomed their mistress every morning and evening, and their restlessness when she left the barn. As the chill grayness of November passed into the cold, snowy sunshine of December, the horses were kept in their stalls most of the time. Michelle worked off some of her nervous energy, and theirs, by riding them around the arena.

With the loss of Sybil, Fatima was failing. Michelle gave her the emotional support that she herself was receiving from her friends. Shortly before Christmas it was necessary to call the vet; Fatima was dying. Mercifully, she did not last long.

One cold, sunny morning, when Michelle had finished her chores, she looked up and saw a big, expensive car coming up the driveway. It stopped, and out stepped Zane, dressed in an ankle-length mink coat and a tall Russian karakul hat. Michelle was wearing muddy boots, a battered sweatshirt with faded lettering that read "BULLS: 1992 WORLD CHAMPIONS," soiled denims, and a CUBS cap." When Zane saw her, she laughed from top to bottom.

"Lordy, me!" Zane exclaimed. "I come to the country to see a country girl, and I see the real thing before my very eyes."

She gave Michelle a hug.

"How ya been, kid?" she asked, "as if I didn't know."

"Come meet Joe," she continued, as an Arab in a flowing white gown stepped out of the car. "I am his property for the day—you know all about that. He is minister of agriculture for some A-rab country where they don't grow anything but oil. He said he wanted to see a farm, so here we are!"

Zane had really come to talk, so she and Michelle sat down for a cup of coffee, while Luke showed the Arab around the farm and buildings. The visitor was impressed by the Arabian horses, which reminded him of his Bedouin boyhood, when he had lived in a tent. When the Arab expressed an interest in fertilizer, Luke took him for a ride on the manure spreader. According to Luke, he enjoyed that most of all.

"Listen up, kid," Zane said. "When Ricky told me that you had married Rex, I couldn't believe it. Rex has been prominent in the gay community in Chicago for years."

Zane noticed a baffled look on Michelle's face, and went on to explain.

"Sometimes gays want to have a regular family, just like they knew when they grew up. So they get married. Nothing wrong with that. That must have been what Rex had in mind. Sometimes it works; sometimes it doesn't. I heard that you are getting an annulment. So how's it been for you? Tough?"

"Zane," Michelle replied, "I'm tired of telling my story. Yes. It has been tough, but I'm feeling better now. What you don't know is how self-centered and inconsiderate Rex is. He put me at death's door. Then I heard him lying about it."

She began crying. "I can go without sex for a while longer," she said. "Looks like I'll have to. But I can't go without love."

Michelle broke down completely, and Zane cradled her in her arms. "I know where you're comin' from, baby," she said. "Meet another one."

And she began crying too.

Just then Thelma entered the room and refilled their cups. They dried their tears, and laughed at each other.

"I don't know which is better," Michelle said, "a good cry or a good laugh!"

"I'll take the combination platter," Zane declared. After that they had a good talk about their days at the Purple Orchid and Elite Escorts.

Zane rose to her full six feet height, with heels.

"Gotta get my A-rab back to town," she said, "Tonight we are going to dinner at a fancy Moroccan restaurant. Do I smell meat loaf bakin' in the kitchen? Gawd, I wish I could stay. I keep askin' Elite Escorts for a plain American who eats meat loaf and other good American stuff, but they keep giving me foreigners. It's amazing what some people will do to get money!"

"I hear you," Michelle replied. "I've been down that road. Thanks for coming. You helped me a lot more than you may realize."

In the meantime, Charley Foxx was preparing to bring Sonny Grubbs to trial for the shooting of Sybil. At first he left Michelle out of his investigation, although he kept his friend, Lawyer Smart, fully informed. Foxx was concerned that Michelle might not wish to reopen old wounds by testifying. He left it to Smart to take care of that.

In early December he called Lawyer Smart.

"Get your client ready to testify," he said. "I've got the bow that killed the horse, and the extra arrows that went with it. With the bow, we were able to find the dealer that sold it, and he put the finger on Sonny. Squirt Peterson had the bow and extra arrows in his apartment. He said he was hiding them for Sonny. He's looking to make a plea bargain on the sexual assault case, but he won't do it until Sonny is in jail. He's scared stiff that Sonny will get him."

"So you're going after Sonny on the horse charge first?" Lawyer Smart asked.

"That's right," Foxx replied. "That means we can hold Sonny until we find a witness to pin the sexual assault on him. Squirt definitely will not talk about that unless he sees Sonny behind bars for a long time."

That same day Foxx filed his case in the circuit court, asking that it be expedited due to other charges that he intended to bring against the defendant. When the court met, Michelle attended as a witness, despite her anxiety at the prospect of seeing Sonny again. Sonny sat sullenly throughout the trial, glaring at Michelle, who carefully avoided his eyes.

The prosecution presented as evidence the bow and arrows, and the proof that Sonny had purchased them. Squirt gave testimony fully implicating Sonny, although he said that he had not been present when the shooting took place.

Michelle testified about the estimated market value of Sybil.

"We have received bona fide offers for Sybil ranging from $12,000 to $16,000," she said, "and never considered them. Sybil and our young stallion were the future of Plainfield. There can be no adequate compensation," she said, "for the value of Sybil to Plainfield Arabians as a brood mare, nor for the personal anguish I have felt at losing her."

Michelle was greatly relieved when Sonny was convicted of criminal damage to property worth more than $10,000, a felony in Illinois. He was confined to the county jail, pending other charges promised by the prosecution.

The next day Michelle appeared at the courthouse and asked to speak to the state's attorney. When she gave her name, the receptionist called Charley Foxx, who appeared immediately. He wore his hat indoors, as well as out, but pushed back on his head.

"I have decided that it is time to tell my story," Michelle said. "The trial yesterday convinced me."

Foxx ushered her into his office, where she told what had happened at the lake.

"You realize," Foxx pointed out, "that if you give evidence in this case, you will have to testify in open court. Bubba and Sonny are popular people in this town, and lots of people in Plainfield owe their living to Bubba Grubbs. In a small town, people's personal knowledge means a lot in a trial."

"I'll take my chances with that," Michelle replied. "The people of Clarksville know me well, and I have lots of friends too."

Foxx continued: "You will be cross-examined by a defense attorney. The party may get rough, although the judge and I will do what we can to keep it civil."

Michelle had never been cross-examined, but she had watched *Perry Mason* and other courtroom dramas on TV, and had a general idea of what to expect.

"I guess I'll just have to take it as it comes," she said.

"Good girl," Foxx replied, looking pleased. "Just tell the truth, and everything will turn out fine."

Foxx decided that the sexual assault case had to go to court, ready or not. He brought charges against Sonny, and was granted an early trial.

On the morning of the trial, people were lined up for several blocks well before the trial began. When the doors to the courthouse opened, they poured in, jostling to find a place to sit. Soon the courtroom was packed, with people standing in the hallway. Bubba Grubbs and his mousey little wife sat with Squirt on the bench behind Sonny and his lawyer.

Exactly at 10:00 a.m. the court was called to order. Judge Theodore Bison took his seat on the bench and reviewed the charge. Sonny, through his lawyer, pleaded "Not guilty."

Foxx knew that most people used the word "rape" loosely, and were not aware of the correct legal terminology. His first step was to establish in the minds of the jurors the legal definition of sexual assault in Illinois.

"What used to be called rape," he said, "is now called criminal sexual assault. The crucial considerations," he said, "are clear indications of intent to inflict a sexual act on an unwilling person, and the use of physical force."

He paused to let his first point sink in.

"That includes any intrusion," he continued, "however slight, of any part of the body of one person—including a finger—into the sex organ of another person."

"Mr. Foxx," the judge interrupted, "I'll explain the law in this courtroom. You present the evidence, and the jury will render the verdict. O.K.?"

Judge Bison, of course, knew Charley Foxx personally. They had been to law school together, and he had been state's attorney before he was elected to the bench. He was determined to conduct a strict trial that left no room for an appeal.

"The important point," Foxx emphasized, ignoring the judge's mild rebuke, "is that the defendant used extreme force against his victim. Only the intervention of others prevented him from accomplishing his purpose, which was to complete an act of sexual intercourse."

Waldo Smart, who was in California, was not called to testify. His testimony would be suspect, because everyone knew that he was the son of Michelle's attorney, who was sitting beside her. Rusty and Clara testified, as did several classmates who were also at the party. None of this testimony added up to a firm case against Sonny.

As Michelle anxiously awaited her turn, the dark thoughts came back. Did she really know what had happened at the party? Did it matter? Did SHE matter? What difference did all of this make? She had spent six months trying to forget. Why torment herself by bringing it all back?

The prosecution depended mainly upon the testimony given by Michelle. She was quaking when called to the witness stand. She forced herself to make eye contact with the jurors; Foxx had told her that eye contact would show confidence in her testimony. She knew many of them personally.

Sonny slouched insolently in his chair, daring her to tell what had happened. Michelle was frightened when she saw him—frightened that he would find some way to get even with her, through surrogates, if not by his own hand.

When Foxx began his questioning, he saw an almost frantic look in Michelle's eyes. She recalled the powerlessness she had felt, as Squirt held her arms and Sonny ripped her clothes from her body.

"Please tell us, Michelle," Foxx asked, "what happened next."

Michelle began to weep softly. Foxx gave her his handkerchief.

"Would you like to take a break?" the judge asked, in a kindly manner.

"No, thank you," Michelle replied, "I don't need a break."

Foxx repeated his question.

"First Sonny pulled down my slacks and panties. Then he put his hand down there," she said, pointing at her crotch.

"Do you have a word for what it is that he touched with his hand?"

Michelle drew a deep breath: "He pushed his finger into my vagina."

"What were you doing?"

"I was struggling to get away. Squirt held both my arms down. Sonny's weight was on my body. His other hand was covering my mouth. I bit it, and when he pulled it away I screamed for help."

Michelle breathed a deep sigh of relief, and relaxed back into her chair. She had said it, and in public. It hadn't been that hard to do, after all. The rest came easily. Confidently, she told how Waldo, Clara, and Rusty had come to help her.

When Michelle had finished, Sonny's lawyer, a hard-boiled defense attorney from Chicago, went at her in cross-examination. He was a heavy-set man, almost bald, with a rough voice and a wolfish grin. He tried to intimidate Michelle into saying things that she didn't mean.

"On direct examination," he said, "you told us that Sonny forced you to engage in activities that you were unwilling to engage in. Right!"

"Yes," Michelle answered, as her anxiety returned.

"You testified that Sonny kissed you, correct?"

"Yes."

"You also said that you resisted when Sonny wanted to go further than you wanted to go?"

An alarm bell rang in Michelle's brain, as she realized what the question implied.

"I didn't want to go anywhere," she replied, firmly. "Sonny kissed me against my will, and I pushed him away."

"Yet the two of you wound up on the ground, and portions of your clothing and Sonny's clothing were removed, isn't that true?"

Foxx had instructed Michelle to answer questions on cross-examination with "Yes" or "No," but most of the defense lawyer's questions were cunningly framed to make that impossible.

Michelle got her back up.

"Sonny did it," she replied, a note of irritation in her voice. "He shoved me to the ground. He pulled my clothes off and unzipped his pants. I resisted as best I could, but he was strong and Squirt was on me too."

"Isn't it true, though, that you did not report being forced into these intimate relations until just recently?"

"Yes."

"So, young lady, you didn't tell anyone because you were embarrassed."

"Partly true."

"And you were embarrassed because both you and Sonny just got carried away?"

"No, that's not true—that's not true—you keep putting words in my mouth!"

Michelle's exasperation was showing, and the defense attorney thought he saw his opportunity to rattle her.

He stepped as close as possible to the witness stand, his big body looming over her.

"You didn't inform the police," he thundered, wagging his index finger in her face, "because you knew that your father would blame YOU!"

Michelle was shocked at the question. She paused a moment.

"I must tell you," she replied softly, "that my father died that night. When I got home I learned that he was dead. I am an orphan."

A hush fell over the courtroom. The defense attorney was taken completely by surprise. No one had informed him of that fact, although everyone on the jury and in the courtroom knew it. He mumbled a statement of regret, but his body sagged as the air went out of his balloon. He knew that his tactless question had deeply offended the members of the jury. He terminated the cross-examination immediately, and Michelle stepped down from the witness stand. Foxx and Smart beamed their approval.

In his summation to the jury, Sonny's attorney returned to the attack, using a common ploy in rape cases—blame the victim.

"Hey," he exclaimed, "these kids were out to raise a little hell. They had just graduated from high school. Those who went there knew what to expect. Who is this accuser to act so innocent? She and the defendant had been steady dates for two years. Everyone knew that. Maybe the defendant got carried away a little, and a scuffle resulted, but—Hey!—that's par for the course. Do you members of the jury—solid citizens, as I can plainly see—have any idea of how kids act these days?"

Before the judge could stop him, he slipped in the fact that Michelle had been a stripper at the Purple Orchid under the false name, Marcella of Carpentersville. He also managed to refer indirectly to her employment at Elite Escorts, which he referred to as a cover for prostitution.

Michelle listened with rising indignation to his distortion of her personal morality and her career as a stripper. She feared that her testimony had been discredited and the case was lost. She could see uncertainty on Foxx's face as he rose to sum up. Sonny and his lawyer gave each other high fives and leaned back in their chairs, confidently.

"The defense has said," Foxx began, "that this case is just a matter of one person's word against another. Well, there's much more to this case than that."

"Yer durn tootin' there is," a shrill, nasal voice rang out. Everyone turned to look. Bubba's wife, a lean, dessicated woman, her leathery cheeks flushed with outrage, had risen to her feet.

"I'm not gonna let this sweet girl be blackened," she exclaimed, "when I can do suffin' about it! Sonny done it. I heerd him and Squirt talkin' about it afore the party. They wuz laffin' and braggin' about what they done when they come home. Sonny has been runnin' amuck, and his Dad has let him do it. Even eggin' him on."

Bubba seized her and tried to stop her, but she broke free from his clutches.

"I hate to testify against my own son," she said, as she jerked her arm backward and gave Bubba an elbow in the face.

"But if suffin' ain't done about Sonny, someday he's gonna kill somebody. Thank you very much for hearin' me out."

Pandemonium broke out in the courtroom. While the defense attorney cried foul, and the judge tried to restore order, Foxx prepared to have the witness sworn in and repeat her testimony.

At that moment Squirt Peterson, as his chance to make a plea bargain evaporated, rose from his seat. He threw himself on the mercy of the court, and declared that he would testify too.

With this new testimony, the jury's verdict was a foregone conclusion. Not until the judge sentenced Sonny to a long term at Stateville Prison in Joliet did Michelle feel safe.

As she drove home to Plainfield, she was confident that her long nightmare was over.

# CHAPTER 12

# *Waldo*

Christmas was lonely for Michelle. When Clara and Rusty invited her to join them, she insisted that they celebrate by themselves their first Christmas as a married couple. Shortly after the trials, Thelma retired and went to Chicago to live with her sister. Michelle was delighted when Thelma called and invited her to spend Christmas Day with them. She was pleased and surprised when Gloria and Biff turned up too.

The bright spot in her near future was the New Years' Eve party of her class at the Holiday Inn. This would be their first time together since the ill-fated party at the lake. Some of her classmates had left for college in the fall, and others had found employment in Chicago and the suburbs, because Clarksville had little to offer.

Michelle felt a tingle of excitement at the possibility that Waldo Smart might be there. He was home for Christmas vacation, Rev. Wiseman told her, with a sly look in his eye. Waldo had not called, but she heard from Clara that he had asked about her.

In the previous six months, Michelle had learned to take charge of her life, and she did so again. She drove into Chicago to one of the dress shops recommended by Rex, where she purchased an expensive little black dress with matching hose and heels. She cleaned the house, vacuumed her car, and baked a batch of cookies.

As she dressed for the party, she took out her mother's diamond necklace and earrings. She decided that she was now ready to wear them. She found her mother's white wool shawl; just right to warm her shoulders on a cold night.

As she looked in the full-length mirror in her bedroom, she pronounced herself ready. Thus prepared, she drove off to the party, and the hoped-for meeting with Waldo.

The ballroom at the Holiday Inn was filled, not only with classmates, but with boyfriends, girlfriends, and in some cases, husbands or wives of the graduates. Michelle had always been popular, but her classmates were taken aback when they saw their tall, confident, poised, and stunningly good-looking classmate.

"Michelle," one girl asked, "what are you doing these days? Are you a model?"

"Michelle, I hardly recognized you," said another. "I thought you were a farm girl. You didn't learn to dress like that riding horses."

Most of the guys were struck dumb. They hardly dared speak to her. "Hey, Michelle," said one, who had already developed the persona that would eventually make him a successful auto dealer, "you're lookin' great, kid." To the irritation of his girlfriend, he added: "Where were you when I was at Clarksville High?"

Michelle saw that most of her classmates looked a lot better than they had in high school. They were better dressed, more poised, and less likely to act up. When the shock of her good looks wore off, she was soon talking with them about the happy times they had enjoyed in high school, and their hopes for the future. By an unstated consensus, no one said anything about the party at the lake, or Sonny Grubbs. Squirt Peterson, who was on probation, decided not to come.

Michelle's heart leaped into her throat when she saw a tall figure with craggy features and an oversize forehead enter the ballroom. He looked around too, expectantly. When their eyes met, they were mature enough not to engage in high-school level coyness.

"Hi, Michelle," Waldo said, confidently, as he approached her. "I hoped you would be here."

"Me too, Waldo," Michelle replied, as she took his arm. It was clear that both intended to spend the rest of the evening together.

Waldo was still not much of a conversationalist, but Michelle had learned at Elite Escorts how to keep a conversation going. Besides, they were seldom alone, since other classmates were eager to join them. They were surprised almost as much by Waldo as by Michelle.

Waldo was obviously uncomfortable in his tux, and his arms were still too long for his jacket. But that didn't seem to matter. He projected a dignity and bearing far different from the clumsy shyness of his days at Clarksville High. He was more outgoing than before, and a good listener. He told about his Internet startup, Waldo.com, which he had begun as a class project at Cal Tech.

As Michelle and Waldo strolled, arm in arm, through the crowd, Waldo's rugged face was often lighted by his infectious, crooked grin. Michelle, eyes sparkling, was a happy, laughing vision of loveliness. As the evening proceeded, Michelle sensed a surprising closeness between herself and Waldo. She knew that Waldo felt it, too.

At midnight, Waldo squeezed Michelle's waist when they sang "Auld Lang Syne," and gave her a shy peck on the cheek.

Michelle didn't want the evening to end.

"Waldo," she said, "would you like to come out to Plainfield and watch the New Year come in around the world? I enjoyed the party, but we haven't really had a chance to get to know each other."

Waldo was quick to agree, and they drove out to Plainfield in Michelle's car, leaving Waldo's in the Holiday Inn parking lot.

At Plainfield, Waldo settled down on the sofa to watch the New Year on TV, while Michelle went into the kitchen to make cocoa.

"What a marvelous world we live in," Waldo called to Michelle. "All those people, around the world, celebrating a new year and a new millennium—all enjoying the present and hopeful for the future."

Waldo had inherited from his father a tendency to elaborate his thoughts. "Who could imagine," he continued, "a hundred years ago, that the world would be in instant communication, sharing this global holiday. Globalization is here to stay, and at Cal Tech we are ahead of the curve."

Michelle did not hear much of what he was saying. She was bringing cocoa and cookies and being careful not to spill.

She put them on the coffee table, poured a cup for Waldo, and sat down on the sofa beside him. As he continued his discourse on globalization, she cuddled close. She heard her body singing the melody of love, just as Rev. Wiseman had foretold. She gave Waldo a few friendly pokes, and leaned forward to look him in the face and give a little whistle.

Waldo realized that he was talking too much. He smiled self-consciously, and gave his attention to her. Michelle could tell that Waldo had something important to say, but was too shy to say it.

"I guess I'll have to pop the question myself," Michelle thought, "and I'll pop it the way I know best."

She rose to her feet and turned on the stereo, already set to Harry James' recording of "I'm in the Mood for Love." Then she stepped shyly to the center of the living room ("not too fast, Honey!"), raising her eyebrows provocatively, as Waldo looked on, wondering what to expect.

Michelle gave him a good look, letting him know that she was in charge. Saucily she tossed her head, shaking her blonde curls. She laughed with delight at Waldo's surprised look, gave him a warm smile, and took off her shawl, dropping it provocatively on the easy chair ("gracefully, Michelle, gracefully"). Slowly she took off the necklace and earrings, placing them on the mantel of the fireplace ("take your time! take your time!"). Then she turned her back, wiggled free of her little black dress ("give 'em plenty of wiggle, that's it!"), and stepped out of it ("dainty steps, Honey, dainty"). She leaned over the coffee table, giving Waldo a good look at her breasts.

At first Waldo was uncomfortable at Michelle's unexpected actions. Then he realized what Michelle was telling him, and responded. He got up from the sofa, and came out from behind the coffee table. Michelle stepped up, unbuttoned his jacket, loosened his tie, and darted away, laughing. She flicked her fanny at him, using the saucy bumps that she had developed at the Purple Orchid.

Waldo was now fully engaged in the game. He slipped out of his jacket, took off his tie, and dropped his trousers.

Michelle was not finished. "Give 'em time," Gloria had said, "the DNA needs time. The erection comes fast, but them little sperms need to be whipped into a frenzy."

Michelle moved to the piano bench and took off her stockings, displaying her long legs ("stretch and kick your legs! Legs, Honey, legs!"). As Waldo reached for her, she tossed her stockings in his face and took refuge behind the easy chair, where she wiggled out of her panties and garter.

By now Waldo had taken off his shirt and shorts. Grinning, he came after her, head down, like Akbar stalking Sybil.

Teasing and giggling, Michelle picked up the shawl and played matador with her crotch ("don't let 'em see it right away"), then flung it away. Michelle saw that his tube was erect and dripping at the tip. It swayed from side to side, as he tried to catch her.

She met Waldo in the middle of the living room. He seized her and they kissed, passionately. Michelle slipped out of his grasp, kicked off her shoes, and stretched out on the sofa, her knees bent and spread apart.

"Come on in, Waldo," she said, "the door is open, the floor is waxed, and the kettle is hot."

Carefully Waldo placed his large body on hers. Michelle reached down and deftly inserted his tube. She felt a sharp little pain at his first thrust, but she was too gloriously happy to mind that. The rush came in a hurry, and they lay there, gasping.

Waldo lifted his head and looked at her. "Well," he said, showing his crooked grin, "I guess this means we gotta get married."

"Yup," Michelle replied, with a happy laugh, "I guess it does."

They moved to Michelle's bedroom and spent the rest of New Year's Eve sharing physical and personal intimacies, falling asleep in each other's arms.

When Michelle awoke, the sun was shining brightly. It was 10:00 a.m. Waldo was already up and dressed and sitting in the living room, reading the newspaper.

"Stanford is in the Rose Bowl today," he said, as she emerged into the living room. "I guess you're a Wisconsin fan."

"I'm not a fan of anyone but you," Michelle said, as she kissed him. Then she disappeared into the kitchen to make breakfast. As she bent over to serve Waldo his scrambled eggs, her robe fell open (possibly intentionally), which led to another spasm of passion.

As they ate cold scrambled eggs and soggy toast, it seemed that the time had come to take a grown-up view of their future life together. Waldo told Michelle that Waldo.com had been highly successful, and was now worth millions. They both had a good laugh when Waldo confessed that he was the unknown investor who had put up $120,000 for the new mortgage at low interest.

"I'm glad to know that my money problems are over," Michelle said. She cast a sideways glance at Waldo and giggled, as she remarked, slyly: "It's amazing what some people will do to get money!"

"Dot.com stocks are high right now," Waldo said. "I think I'll sell out. I want to come back to Clarksville and live at Plainfield with you. I didn't care much for the West Coast."

"Goody, goody," Michelle cooed, "I hoped you would say that. But what will you do here?"

"I've been thinking of enrolling at Northern Illinois University Law School," Waldo replied, "and going into practice with my Dad."

"I see," said Michelle, "the DNA is doing its work."

Waldo seemed baffled by that remark, but Michelle continued.

"I have DNA too," she said. "My DNA is telling me to take this horse business seriously. There is a program in Equestrian Studies at Black Hawk Community College, west of here at Rock Island. If you can arrange your classes so you can look after the horses a couple days a week, I really should get into that program."

With an unexpectedly bright future ahead of her, Michelle was able to consider possibilities that had been put aside during the previous six months.

"You know, Waldo," she mused, "when I was in grade school, my goal was to compete in the Olympic Games. Mom encouraged me, but when she died, that was the end of that. There is a riding school at Moose River, Minnesota. This summer I'd like to go there for a couple of weeks of intense training. I probably wouldn't make it to the Olympic Games, but I'd like to try equestrian competition anyway."

Michelle thought it best not to mention that she knew Roger and Susan Torgerson, who operated the school.

"Whoa, wait a minute," Waldo exclaimed. "Remember, you're going to be a married lady, and"—recalling the joys of the previous night—"maybe a Mom."

"A Mom!" Michelle exclaimed. "I'd love that!" She pinched his cheek and laughed. "You could look after the baby while I train."

Suddenly Waldo remembered that he hadn't called his parents to tell them where he was. By that time, they were back from church and getting ready for Sunday dinner. Understandably, Mrs. Smart was worried,

"He always called before," she said.

"Now, now, Mother," Lawyer Smart replied. "When these young people leave home, they're on their own. Waldo will call when he is ready."

When Waldo told them that he was at Plainfield, and he and Michelle wanted to get married as soon as possible, the Smarts were delighted. Mrs. Smart invited them to come into town and have dinner, but Michelle frantically signaled "no, no."

"Waldo," she said, "the horses! I forgot the horses."

Quickly she changed into her denims and hurried to the stables. Waldo followed, still wearing his tux.

"I'll help," he said. "This tux has stuff on it, and will have to go to the cleaners, anyway."

Since it was New Years Day, Luke had not come to work that morning. The horses were hungry and thirsty and upset. They knew that something unusual had been going on up at the house. The glow on Michelle's face convinced them that all was well, although they wondered about Waldo. Fatima could have explained it to them. Akbar was dubious. He sensed a rival, and made a considerable racket in his stall before settling down to eat his oats.

When they were finished, Michelle called Rev. Wiseman, who also rejoiced at the news.

"I heard my body singing the melody of love," Michelle exclaimed, "just as you said it would."

As soon as all legal requirements were met, Michelle and Waldo were married at the First Lutheran Church of Clarksville by a beaming Rev. Wiseman. Uncle Jim proudly gave the bride away. Clara, now bulging at the seams, was matron of honor, and Rusty was the best man. Dr. Carey was his usual smiling, bobbing self, but he brought his little black bag with him, and kept a close eye on Clara. The Smarts came with a covey of uncles, aunts, and cousins that Waldo hadn't seen for years. Charley Foxx turned up, wearing his hat as usual during the reception, although he took it off for the wedding ceremony. Grandma and Grandpa came from Philadelphia. The fact that Waldo had been admitted to a distinguished West Coast university was all that Grandma needed to give her blessing.

Of course, Luke and Lena were there, and Ben, wearing an old black suit that nobody present had ever seen before. Biff brought Thelma and Gloria in his 1979 Buick. Thelma cried. Zane turned up wearing a magnificent African gown. She had a cheerful, rosy-cheeked liquor distributor from Oregon in tow.

"This afternoon is free," she whispered to Michelle. "He's payin' for tonight. We're goin' to Michael Jordan's restaurant to have pork chops, American fries, and apple pie a la mode."

There was a large turnout from the congregation and the community. The Dullard brothers, who also were caterers, served refreshments in the church basement.

When the wedding and reception were finished, Michelle and Waldo returned to Plainfield to take care of the horses. Before they left, they told Grandma and Grandpa that they would include Philadelphia in their honeymoon, if they could find time to take one. All the guests agreed that the newlyweds were likely to live happily ever after.

0-595-29026-4